DEVON C. FORD
ABANDONED
TOY SOLDIERS

AETHON BOOKS

ABANDONED

©2019 DEVON C. FORD

Dedicated to Baby J, who at the time of writing this was trying to recreate the chest-bursting scene from Alien...

PREFACE

All spelling and grammar in this book is UK English except for proper nouns and those American terms which just don't anglicize.

PROLOGUE

"Unidentified vessel, this is the USS McAllister," came a voice over the crackling radio in an accent the captain of the ship had never heard outside of a television set, "you are ordered to heave-to immediately and return to port. I repeat, heave-to immediately. We will not allow you to enter deep water."

Captain Mike Xavier, tall and lean but more powerful than his frame suggested, turned and surveyed the people assembled on the bridge of his large transport ship, with his piercing eyes made more prominent as they sat between a thick, dark beard and an equally thick mop of unruly hair. Despite the vessel's huge size, he had very little space for people on board, so whatever indoor areas that could be fashioned into accommodation had been hastily rigged up, and supplies had been stockpiled from wherever they could be found. They had been stolen mostly, but he believed in the needs of the many.

He had close to four hundred souls on his ship, curiously named the *Aunt Margaret* but known affectionately by her crew as *The Maggie,*

and he had been one of the few to emerge as a natural leader in the areas far from London and the initial outbreak.

When the news reports went inexplicably dark and nobody knew what was happening, he and his crew had picked up their heavy engineering wrenches and crowbars, and they'd defended the docks from the looters who ran riot in the centre of Liverpool.

A week after that initial panic, new sounds rent the air over the oddly picturesque, industrial Albert Docks. Those sounds were of terror, of bloodlust and the primal fear of prey unable to escape a predator. Ahead of that wave of fear came the refugees; those human beings in possession of self-preservation instincts more attuned than others.

Xavier made an instant decision, regardless of whether it was right or wrong, but he made the decision to help by admitting them into their safe enclave, even before he knew what they were running from.

His men blinked, wide-eyed in disbelief at the instructions, but a growled order for them to move their arses was quickly obeyed.

Over the next month they had fortified the docks, saving people whenever they could and using their tools day and night to clear the strong fences surrounding the commercial docks of the undead. Had they not heard the accounts of those desperate people running through the open gates as those inside shouted them on, they might not have believed what came from the city to gnaw at the chain link barrier in an unthinking bid to mindlessly devour the survivors. Xavier had left one of his more senior men in charge of the gate, a big French deck hand called Jean-Pierre, with arms like knotted and tarred ropes, and shiny, olive skin, and he showed his men how to lead the zombies away from the gates and put them down quietly.

Les morts, he called them. The dead. And Jean-Pierre believed that the dead should be treated with respect, even if they were trying to eat them.

"Unidentified vessel, unidentified vessel, this is the USS McAllister. We are a US Navy Frigate with a full complement of armaments. We are authorized and fully prepared to use deadly force if you do not heave-to immediately and return to port. There will be no further verbal warnings. Heave-to *now.*"

Xavier, the son of a French merchant sailor and a local pub landlady, a native of the city and a man who had been on those docks since he was a boy, snatched up the binoculars on the side of the instrument panel on his bridge, and scanned the horizon off to his right.

He found the vessel, tiny in comparison to his own gargantuan freighter, and watched as it continued heading west under power and most certainly not heaving-to. He didn't hear the double crump sounds of far-off deck guns firing a single shot each into the path of the commercial boat, but he saw the huge geysers of sea water erupt skywards in answer.

"Fucking hell," he cursed to himself, the binoculars still glued to his eyes as he saw the two plumes of white water erupt directly in the path of the vessel, "go back, for God's sake, man," he said in a low voice, willing the unknown boat's captain to turn back and not risk the lives on everyone on board.

The other captain, whoever it was, tested the patience of the US Navy officer, who gave his orders and showed anyone observing that he wasn't backing down. The warning shots were the last message, albeit not a verbal one, and Xavier had a sinking feeling about what was going to happen next.

Dropping the binoculars and putting himself back inside the confines of the bridge, he gave a simple order to his helmsman.

"All ahead stop," he said solemnly, "bring us about."

His helmsman responded with naval terminology betraying his roots, and the ship gave the smallest of lurches as their forward momentum was cut. The sheer size of his vessel and the massive displacement of water it created made it very diffi-cult to feel the changes, but Xavier knew his *Maggie* well.

Even before they began their slow turn to take themselves away from the distant, loose blockade that their ship's radar had warned them about, everyone on the bridge sitting high up at the stern of the big vessel started to watch, not needing the binoculars. They saw the explosion and its accompanying fire-ball as the bright orange ball spewed a great cloud of black smoke into the air.

Nothing was said after the initial shouts and screams of alarm, but the atmosphere on the ship was one of frustration and fear.

Picking the lesser of the two evils, they sailed back towards the docks and back towards the uncertain safety of north west England.

CHAPTER

ONE

Squadron Sergeant Major Dean Johnson's detached unit of light reconnaissance tanks and armoured personnel carriers had exhausted their supply of ammunition into the left flank of the massive horde of undead heading straight for their island stronghold. That horde looked for all the world as though the entire human contents of a large city had all decided to walk in one direction at the same time and with no discernible purpose. It had, however, been degraded by over a quarter of its original number by the attack of a troop of four German main battle tanks. But the dead had piled up so high that the majority of the swarm had simply marched onwards and ignored them. That barrier of broken bodies prevented their advance and forced them to try and find another way around, but that delay had effectively removed them from the fight.

Johnson's convoy, under the command of Captain Palmer, had been returning from London where they had rescued an eight-man special forces team and the scientist they had been sent in to extract. That extraction had fallen foul of another swarm, another inexplicable gathering of the dead that were known to form and dissipate without obvious sense or reason.

And even though that swarm was only a tiny fraction of the size of the one that had cut off their retreat, it was still large enough to make the tight confines of the city streets an impassable death trap.

The armour had rolled in, snatched up their objectives, and rolled out with relative ease, but on their return journey they had been forced to stop and send their precious human cargo out by helicopter. Those objectives, the scientist and his box of virus samples, were escorted out by half of the special forces soldiers in the form of a four-man Special Boat Service (SBS) patrol. They had flown south, out over the Jurassic coast of southern England and into the Channel where the remnants of the military and government command hierarchy remained and pulled whatever strings they had left at their disposal; which, tragically, weren't that many.

The return of the convoy to their commandeered island base just off the coast was delayed by mechanical failures. They had to abandon the damaged tracked vehicles in order to keep moving and get into the fight, and they had arrived just in time to pour machine gun and 30mm cannon fire into the massed bodies heading for the causeway which cut them off from their people. The defenders on the island had brought tonnes of their own lead and explosives to bear on the attack from the remainder of the squadron's guns, as well as the two stranded Chieftain tanks that brought them not only heavy cannons, but also their new commanding officer in the Captain.

The biggest weapons deployed in the fight were both unexpected and unrequested, as the American Navy destroyer had steamed towards the coast at full speed to bring both of their huge deck guns, their 127mm cannons firing high explosive rounds, to bear. However, as helpful as their unexpected assistance had been, it had also ultimately spelled disaster.

Their final salvo before the big guns ceased their bombardment had struck the bridge itself, which connected the supports of the narrow causeway, their only way on and off the raised spit of land they had called home for close to a month. The bridge had collapsed, almost costing the lives of the entire tank crew who were the armed and armoured roadblock. They survived that, but the three men who had escaped the fifty-five-tonne coffin were forced to watch as their driver failed to make it out.

Although cut off from the mainland by that final ordnance, it was actually the salvo immediately before that which caused the real problems. One explosive round, detonating deep within the attacking mass of dead, blew scattered body parts outwards in a huge half-sphere of gore and ruin. Some of that re-animated flesh landed on the island, including one shattered chunk of meat and bone that was wrapped in the remnants of grey overalls with an embroidered logo that was illegible from the black gunk that had leaked into the fabric. That fabric obscured the ragged diagonal tear across the chest, leaving one complete shoulder and arm that was oddly untouched by the destruction wrought on the rest of the body. The head, although scorched on the side where the bright white stump of an upper arm bone wiggled inside a shoulder joint exposed by the scoured flesh, remained fully animated as it thrashed around, trying to free itself from the confines of the clothing.

That in itself would not have spelled disaster, only it had been one of the faster, smarter ones. What some of the people on the island called the Leaders, what the Royal Marines called *Limas,* and what others had no name for because they had underestimated not only their faster movements, but also their unexplained ability to think.

Whereas every other shambolic, shuffling corpse was slow-moving and relatively simple to dispatch individually or in small groups, the faster ones displayed something resembling guile. This particular one, or at least the half a torso, head and one arm of it, freed itself from the restraint of what had been the last outfit it had ever put on, back when it had been a man and not a monster, and spun its head around, trying to get a fix on the myriad sounds echoing around the battle.

"Five left," shouted a hoarse voice from directly ahead, making the burnt and blackened face fix on the source of the sound, and lock its milky eyeballs onto a target.

"More ammo!" cried the voice louder now, sending a man back to fetch more 51mm mortar rounds to lob high over the now severed road bridge and into the mass. They still kept coming, only to pour over the destroyed parapet and into the fast-moving current to be swept away in the same direction of the stinging smoke from their burning white phosphorous smoke bombs.

As the fourth of those five remaining bombs popped out of the tubes and shot skywards, the hand of the animated piece of burnt meat had clawed forwards using the gaps in the old stonework of the roadway to gain purchase and propel it onwards. Just as the last mortar round was dropped into the hot metal pipe to send it far away at an impossible speed, that hand reached out and locked onto the webbing belt of the soldier kneeling beside the weapon with his back to the unseen threat. He screamed, crying out involuntarily in fright, as he fell backwards with the pull and kicked out the leg of the man holding the mortar tube, sending the bomb with its armed fuse directly into a nearby building through a tall window. It exploded and poured smoke out of the shattered glass. Men screamed and shouted all around as they burned and panicked, but one scream overrode them all.

The man who had been hauled back by what transpired to be just under a quarter of a former human being felt a desperate and strong hand clamp over his face, the sharp fingernails digging in for grip and finding the soft recess of his left eye socket and the vulnerable eyeball within. As that nail punctured the skin and drove deeply inside the skull behind the eye, he bellowed a high-pitched shriek of shock and agony. That shriek was quickly stifled when cold teeth clamped down on the warm flesh of his neck and burst the blood vessels beneath, before the skin gave way and a huge chunk of flesh came sinuously free. Blood pulsed out onto the stone in massive, arterial gushes, soaking victim and attacker and painting them both the same colour.

The other man of that mortar team had fled as soon as he knew that the white phosphorous bomb would land inside their own lines, and as he didn't like the thought of having his skin burned off his back at a temperature of five thousand degrees, he simply ran.

The battle was being fought on two fronts by then; the enemy advancing towards the thirty-foot wide gap in the roadway were still being fired on as the mass of dead were clogging up even the deep, fast moving coastal water and piling up on the nearest bit of sandy edge to the island, where their numbers would eventually break any but the stoutest of obstacles. The rest of the efforts of the living were spent in evacuating injured men from the building that was now burning violently, and they were carried and dropped some distance away as their rescuers went back to save men and equipment from the flames that by now reached high above the pitched roof.

A groan to the left of the quarter-zombie caught its attention, making it perform the same grotesque travel by clawing its own remains across the cobblestones to find the source. That source was four men, two of whom writhed and moaned; one merely emitted a series of long, intense grunts, as if he were screaming inside in a dream from which he couldn't wake, and the closest to the zombie simply lay still.

It didn't know how it knew, but some instinct or smell or other sense told it that this man was already dead and was simply not registering as food when there was moving prey nearby. But the body did present itself as a reliable handhold with which the crawling nightmare could haul itself over to fall on the three wounded men, who, as loud as their screams were, could not raise the alarm over the cacophony of war and flame and smoke.

By the time those three men had bled to death from the cruel bites to their throats and forearms and wrists and hands and faces, the first soldier to have fallen prey opened its milky eyes and sat up to search for fresh meat of its own.

"Attack rear! Attack rear!" came the panicked shout of one man, who was fumbling with the Sterling sub machine gun in his shaking hands. But his frantic shouts went unheard as he fell victim to his friend of many years, who in that instant, did not recognise him as anything but food.

By the time the firing to the front had faded away and those soldiers at the front of the line, led by Lieutenant of Marines Chris Lloyd, had been reorganised and moved on to defend the beach, there were six fully-mobile zombies hunting men in the rear of their forces, thanks to the impossibly damaged remains of just one man. There were shouts and gunfire from the waterline below them, but the higher-pitched screams of women further up the island's incline grabbed the attention of three of the zombies, who began shambling their way uphill and into the undefended streets filled with civilians.

Cut off, under attack from the water and with a growing enemy gathering strength from within their own enclave, the people left behind on the island were doomed.

CHAPTER

TWO

Peter and Amber had huddled together as an unseasonably chill wind ripped across the coastline. She had listened to the music on his cassette player until the batteries wore down, to then play the songs in slow-motion, she hugged the limp and dirty stuffed lamb up under her chin and sat in her characteristically quiet manner. It wasn't cold inside their new home, even with having to leave a small window open so that the cat who had decided the two small humans belonged to it could come and go as it pleased. But the whistling wind made them both feel insecure and forced them upstairs, where they sat with their knees drawn up and quilts wrapped around them, just waiting for the night to end.

Part of that collective feeling of unease was the hour of booming noise in the distance that began like thunder and ended like the ceaseless banging of multiple drums, until no single sound was distinguishable from another. Those sounds had dropped suddenly in their intensity, as though the bass drum had simply stopped working, then the other sounds faded away to echoes of nothing. Still, they sat quietly upstairs in the big house they had taken over and each drifted deep into their own thoughts before sleep took them.

Peter replayed the events of that day over and over in his head, of how he had truly known terror like he had never experienced in his life when he thought that he had failed Amber, and that she would be killed by the zombie that had caught them unprepared in the house they were searching for supplies. He was sure, or at least he hoped, that she did not know how close she had come to being failed by him and being eaten; torn apart in blood and screams.

He again thanked whatever it was up there looking out for him and giving him his streak of luck, which, he had to admit, was still teetering on the side of good, given that he, that *they*, were still alive.

He had guessed that the rolling thunder was some form of battle raging in the distance, but since he felt he had no place among the grown-ups left behind after everything went wrong, he decided that seeking out their assistance wasn't a priority for him and his ward.

And, he thought logically, *if the army, or whoever, are in the middle of a battle, then they're probably worse off than we are.*

After they had made it back to their new place and dragged the last of four cartloads inside to stockpile their plundered resources, Peter had allowed himself to replay the recent events, and paid special attention to the minute details his mind conjured up about the last three monsters he had killed with his pitchfork and spike. Two of those, he hated to accept, were conquered by sheer luck.

The female zombie who had walked into the house where he had first found Amber, the woman who used to be a nurse, or who at least dressed like one, had moved faster than he'd expected, and only his good fortune had pinned her snapping jaw shut as he missed her brain with the weapon. He had pulled his back-up, his spike made from an off-cut of the pitch-fork, and he'd managed to kill it, but he'd felt then that it was too close for comfort. He hadn't had time to consider the what-ifs of that scenario, because he had convinced the young girl to come with him and flee the village, ranging over low hills and fields until they found somewhere safer to be.

The other two had been dispatched only hours before; the first a naked, bloated and repulsive creature rising from the low, green water of a brook. He'd been crossing the small bridge and had not even seen it until Amber's curious and eerie warning had made him turn back to look at her. The memory brought with it the smell, and his stomach flipped angrily as it threatened to show him the can of soup he'd had earlier.

Shaking that away, his mind brought back the slow-motion action replay of the last person, no, the last *zombie,* he had killed. That one terrified him the most, not for fear of his own violent death and dismemberment, but for the fact that the thing was reaching out for Amber when his run of good luck had struck again, and the tip of his pitchfork, thrust out ahead of him as he fell, punctured the spine of the thing and paralysed it from the neck down.

Amber seemed unperturbed by this, and he reckoned that she didn't know how close she had come to getting killed. He knew that she didn't realise he had fallen over the raised edge of a rug and nearly ended her life through sheer clumsiness, and he had no plans to tell her. Ever.

He'd been doing fine for a few weeks after his miserable existence on the family farm came to an uninspiring but utterly bowel-loosening, terrifying conclusion. He had been driven off his land by a crowd of zombies, a crowd larger than all the people he had ever seen before in one place together. He had been quietly going from house to house, moving at night and sneaking into the quaint country homes to eat whatever tinned food they had, and drink the water left in their taps. He didn't understand why some houses still had running water when others did not, but in terms of priorities he decided that it didn't really matter.

That quiet drifting had lasted until he was woken one daytime by men in a car who had dragged away a woman from a cottage opposite his hiding place, leaving behind his new purpose in life in the form of a crying, terrified girl.

He had been happy just looking after himself, but that existence had been pointless, other than to simply remain alive until something changed. As a rule, he avoided any other people, alive or dead, but now that he had a child to look after, he felt differently about everything.

Amber, all four and three-quarter years old of her, was more than half of his own age, as he wouldn't turn ten for another month, but that age difference was relative and circumstantial. He was old enough to protect her, so he did just that.

Add to that the responsibility of the cat who had followed them for miles from their last hiding place, and his need to be on the lookout for cat food, as well as anything that could sustain them, and Peter felt in that moment more than a little overwhelmed by life.

It had always been his sister who had looked out for him, who had protected him and not told him about the dangers of life, because he was too young to have to face them. Now, following that model, he became that person for Amber, who could not protect herself.

Standing up as quietly as he could, because she had finally fallen asleep, Peter tiptoed down the stairs and into the dark, open-plan ground floor of the modern house. It was dark because they had tightly drawn all of the curtains on the front and upstairs rear of the house, leaving the long, wide picture windows of the kitchen uncovered as that was overlooked by nothing, and he'd decided it was safe to leave that way.

A small window beside the back door, one high up and too small for a person to climb through, was left open as a means for their four-legged follower to use as access. Pet wasn't the right word for it, as no person can ever claim to truly *own* a cat, as the species practically invented the word capricious. Nevertheless, it had followed them and stayed with them, if only for the fact that Peter used the magic tin opener and fed the black and brown cat a meal that it didn't have to hunt first, while avoiding the foul-smelling, slow-moving humans who seemed to want to grab it every time they saw it. Peter was happy for the cat because each night they had been together, it had reappeared at some point and was always curled up on or next to Amber whenever they woke.

When it realised they were awake, it would purr loudly, like marbles rolling around inside a hard leather case, and it would nuzzle the girl until she giggled.

The sound of her laugh cut through his soul every time he heard it, as though that sound alone was the only thing worth going through their daily routine for.

As soon as he walked into the kitchen and gently turned the tap to run cold water into a glass, a noise sounded at the window and Peter's head whipped to the side to see the animal teetering on the frame, half in and half out of the house. It meowed at him, rolling the sound into a chirping gargle before dropping down with a thud onto the worktop and then to the floor in stages as it trotted to his feet with a raised tail curled over at the tip like a question mark. The rattling purr wound up to full intensity and he stepped carefully over the cat to pick up a tin of the smelly meat chunks in gravy, and he opened it to stop the noise and the nagging which snaked between his ankles in a ceaseless figure-eight.

He put the dish on the kitchen bench and watched as the

cat sniffed at the meal, then looked back at him to emit a croaky meow and step lightly to the tap which was still dripping from when he'd run himself the glass of water. It fussed at the tip of the tap, turning its head and licking at it to force a small dribble of liquid to run out, which it lapped at.

"You thirsty?" Peter asked it, speaking more to himself, but seeing the cat respond to his words with another chatter of dry-throated meowing. He opened three cupboards in turn, looking for something appropriate and finding a small, glass cooking dish which he filled with water from the tap. The cat stepped with one paw onto his forearm to begin drinking as the tap still ran and made it awkward for Peter to hold the dish until he managed to put it down near the food.

He watched, sipping his own water, as the cat lapped desperately at the cool liquid to slake a thirst the boy hadn't thought to predict. When it had finished, it sat down and wiped a paw over its face to clear away the droplets attached to the fur on its snout, before dropping down again to trot across the tiled floor, tail raised in the characteristic curl, and up out of the window again.

Peter thought about the brook and the only natural source of water he had seen in the small village, deciding that the cat probably didn't want to drink from it because of the rotten corpse contaminating it.

He took his water to the wide corner settee in the open lounge area, shrouded in late afternoon gloom with the curtains drawn, and he sat. The thunder, or the guns as he had guessed they were, had stopped hours since to leave a menacing memory, and the air outside had taken on an ominous silence, with the exception of the gusts of wind which howled in fits and bursts. He knew he would have to wake Amber up soon, to make her some food from their newly-acquired stocks that were piled neatly on the kitchen benches in order of category.

As long as they didn't attract the attention of any crowds of the monsters passing through, and as long as none of the other houses in the village held unwelcome surprises of more than one or two, or worse still, the faster ones who seemed to collect a gang of the others around them, he guessed they could stay there for weeks.

If they were lucky.

THREE

Corporal Daniels, sitting inside the ungainly but more spacious static armoured vehicles, their remaining Sultan, tried repeatedly to get a response on the radio until a hand rested on his arm. Turning to the big man in the small seat beside him, his Squadron Sergeant Major shook his head once at him. The sudden silence was replaced by a muted and weak banging sound from outside their hull, making the four men crammed inside freeze and listen. A faint moan drifted to them, telling them instantly what was outside, looking for a way in.

Their mixed convoy now comprised a single tracked Spartan, their command vehicle of the Sultan with its oddly configured taller profile, two of the brutish and rugged Saxons, which contained Maxwell and his two crews from the abandoned Spartans, and a four-man Special Air Service patrol, as well as their four remaining Fox armoured cars of Strauss' One Troop.

Thirty-one men, squeezed into eight of their original ten vehicles and dangerously short on ammunition after pouring lead into the disgusting, roiling mass of decaying bodies, now sat in silence inside their armoured hulls, and they waited.

Waiting was something they were accustomed to, only not in those specific circumstances. Anyone in any branch of the military would be intimately acquainted with the concept of hurrying up and waiting, but none had ever faced any concept of danger anywhere near their current stress levels.

They waited for an order, waited for something to do and to feel useful. The sounds of moans and bodies bumping into their vehicles echoed and sowed the seeds of panic and fear amongst them. Only a few men held their nerve convincingly, and four of those were in the rear of one Saxon personnel carrier. Major Downes, officer commanding the SAS patrol and referred to simply as Boss by his three men, regarded the rest of his small detachment.

Mac had his eyes closed, but Downes knew he would not be sleeping. Even if he was, he knew that the man would come awake instantly and be fully combat effective inside of a second. Beside him, and similarly motionless, was Smiffy, and to Downes' left was Dez, who was slowly and quietly checking the action of the dismounted general purpose machine gun, or *gimpy*, taken from one of the abandoned Spartans. He evidently liked the weapon, but being the patrol's demolitions expert, it came as no surprise that he held a reverence bordering on an inappropriately romantic involvement with a weapon so capable of destruction. His fingers ran over the linked ammunition for it with a light caress; part technical assessment and part suspect eroticism.

The weapon was undoubtedly a serious piece of kit, and indeed their own vaunted regiment had demonstrated that a single belt of two hundred rounds of the heavy 7.62 ammunition could be used to create a doorway in a brick wall. In polar-opposite contrast, their personal weapons were the small-calibre suppressed version of Germany's best mass-produced sub machine gun, the Heckler & Koch MP5SD. Spitting their lethally accurate 9mm projectiles with a coughing sound and able to fire in single shot, three-round burst and fully automatic modes, it made them a perfect weapon for close-quarters battle with the undead, who seemed to demonstrate an unnerving ability to locate their prey by sound alone.

The noises made by the few undead pawing over their vehicles outside didn't bother them as it wasn't their problem to deal with yet, but that wasn't to say that they weren't aware of the threat, in case it became their focus in the near future.

In the command vehicle directly behind them, Captain Palmer and Squadron Sergeant Major Johnson exchanged a look. It was instigated by the young officer, and it asked for ideas as to what the hell they should do next.

They were desperately low on ammunition, unable to raise anyone on the island or anywhere else for that matter, and they had to make a decision. That decision hinged on whether the island had been overrun or not, but to find out they would be forced to leave the safety of their armour.

Using the viewports available to him, Palmer tried to count how many Screechers, as their detachment of mixed forces called them, were in their immediate area.

"Retreat a few hundred metres," Johnson suggested in a low voice, seeing no response to his words from the officer, other than his fingers moving to switch the channels on his radio to address the convoy.

"Withdraw, minimum three hundred metres," he ordered, hearing the engines of the different vehicles bark and growl into whistling, clattering life as gears engaged with heavy, mechanical, clunking noises and engine pitches rose to a high whistle before they performed turns and drove away from the wide swathes of broken dead.

Sergeant Strauss, commanding the Fox scout car at the rear of the column, pointed out a raised bluff of ground ahead and to their right, which could accommodate his troop to provide all-around cover. Occupying that position, alien to the warfare he had trained for, to give any attacking force a clear view of their silhouettes, but far more sensible for fighting the new biting, unthinking infantry they had been forced to rapidly adapt to, Strauss opened his hatch and scanned the landscape below them.

The scene was utterly repulsive and stomach-churning. It was horrifying to behold the incredible, destructive power of their guns, which had spread shattered and ruined bodies over almost a mile of flat ground, all the way to the huge mounds of zombies

laid to waste by the combined might of tanks and shore

bombardment. Strauss was torn between a perverse pride in what they could do against vast numbers of enemy infantry, and yet simultaneously sickened by the unnecessary waste of life. His only blessing, he knew from unwelcome experience, was that he was not close enough to truly experience the smell.

Physically shaking his head to force his thoughts to return to the task in hand, he transmitted a report for the benefit of their commanders below.

"Approx. thirty Screechers in close," he said, estimating the numbers of undead who had shambled their way towards the retreating armour, "no Limas."

"Roger, Foxtrot-One-Zero, stand by to engage enemy," Captain Palmer's voice came back before it was interrupted by another transmission.

"Cancel, cancel," it said intently, "Charlie-One-One to last callsign: confirm enemy numbers and confirm negative Limas, over."

Charlie-One-One, Strauss guessed, was the unit callsign for the SAS team currently sitting in the dark rear of a Saxon below his elevated position. Looking back towards the shambling attack, he responded with, "Stand by, Charlie-One-One," and double-checked his numbers and his assessment of their capabilities. Moments later he gave the report more concisely.

"Hello, Charlie-One-One, this is Foxtrot-One-Zero. Confirmed negative for Limas, enemy at six-zero yards and closing. Count thirty-two, confirm three-two, over."

"Roger, all units hold fire, repeat *hold fire*, Charlie-One-One going foxtrot," came the confident and slightly harsh response.

Almost every man in their convoy had been to Northern Ireland and all had trained for that theatre, and all of them knew what *going foxtrot* meant. The four SAS men were going outside to bring the fight to the enemy on foot, and their reason for doing so was solely to keep things quiet.

Inside the back of the Saxon, Downes replaced the phone handset with its inbuilt press-to-talk function and nodded to Trooper Williams, the Yeomanry man assigned as their driver from Maxwell's troop. Turning to his three men, he saw them all readying themselves and their weapons. Dezzy looked momentarily forlorn as he gently set down the long machine gun and drew back the bolt on his MP5 to see the glint of brass in the dim light of the Saxon's interior.

Waiting until six eyes looked up at him for the order to break out, Downes nodded again once and growled the words, "Let's do this."

The dull afternoon light lit up the interior as the rear doors were thrown open and the men filed out in no desperate hurry. It wasn't as though they had to flee the truck and find hard cover to protect themselves from culvert bombs or enemy fire, but Williams marvelled at how rapidly their ingrained training had adapted to a different way of life and death.

The last man turned back and shut the door, pausing as he was about to close it, and leaned his head back inside to fix the driver with a stern look.

"I'll be *back! Hah!*" he said, as he barked a laugh and shut the door, casting the interior back into darkness.

Downes ignored Smiffy's levity, knowing that trying to stop

the man making jokes was as effective as trying to tie knots in snot.

"Spread out, cover in pairs, don't take chances," he said unnecessarily, knowing and trusting the men to do precisely what was required and not to take stupid risks. That was often, he found at least, the biggest misconception about the men in his regiment; they weren't unstable and insane risk-takers with no fear of death, they were just fiercely fit and committed individuals whose personal limits were higher than those of the average person. They were usually cold, methodical, tough men who lived to do their jobs, and that was why they got the best missions, the best kit, and existed outside of the stiff regime of the big green army machine.

Instinctively breaking off into pairs as testimony to the thousands of hours spent in training, one covering and one moving, Mac dropped in behind Downes' shoulder and they stalked forwards to close the gap between themselves and the shuffling zombies. Dez and Smiffy spread out to their left, mirroring their movements. After an advance of thirty paces to halve the gap between vehicles and zombies, their weapons began to cough the small bullets at the heads of the shambling attackers, bullets ripping into open maws to destroy brain stems and 'render them safe' with next to no noise.

"Stoppage!" Downes heard to his left in the unmistakable accent of his Londoner, Smiffy. He didn't need to look, but he knew that Dez would already be standing over him, his left lower leg pressed into Smiffy's back as he physically let him know he was there, covering him as he knelt and cleared his weapon. If he couldn't clear it quickly, or the enemy advanced too close, then he would call out and rise up to draw his secondary weapon and start popping heads with the Browning Hi-Power holstered on his right hip. That would be less than ideal, as only one of them had managed to find a suppressor for their sidearm and that was Downes with his Sig Sauer P228.

"Clear!" Smiffy called. Again, Downes didn't look, because he was still selecting targets and firing three-shot bursts into torn and rotting faces, but he knew that Dezzy would have stepped aside and removed the contact from his partner's back, allowing him the space to stand up safely to rejoin the fight,

Less than a minute into their encroaching action and the loose attacking formation they faced was down. In turn, each man of their respective pairs took turns to perform a tactical reload, when they clicked a fresh magazine of 9mm rounds into their guns, regardless of whether the current load was fully expended. The partially empty magazines went down the front of their dark smocks to be retrieved and refilled later.

"One more," Mac warned in his characteristically dour voice, made even more dolorous by the Scottish accent. All eyes shot forward, and all widened as they realised the last one approaching them wasn't shambling or stumbling, but it seemed to be jogging in a slightly drunken fashion.

"Fucking Lima," Mac warned, with more intensity in his voice, then dropped to one knee and flicked the fire selector of his own weapon from semi-auto to three-shot and began squeezing off bursts to bring it down before it got to them. The others joined him, two firing bursts and two firing longer streams of automatic fire until the thing stumbled and clattered to the roadway twenty paces from them. Loud cracks echoed to their ears as the thing broke bones in the tumbling fall, for it to land, skidding on its face on the tarmac. The four men rose, never taking their eyes off their attacker and the surrounding landscape, as the thing emitted a shrieking groan and rose on its hands to try and get to its feet. One foot, the leg damaged irreparably by either the gunfire or the fall, faced backwards and as it tried to get upright, the bones crunched again, bright white shards puncturing the skin and clothing grotesquely, until it slammed back down to its face to crack its nose and leak black, thick gore from the nostrils, which dripped into an oily puddle before it. The thing began to crawl towards them on three limbs faster than it had any earthly right to do, like some reincarnation of the *Exorcist*.

As one, the three men took an involuntary step backwards and raised their weapons to crouch into the short stocks and take aim. Downes lowered his MP5 and stepped out ahead of the line, making the others drop the ends of their muzzles and display their ingrained respect for the killing power of guns. Stepping forwards confidently into the path of the crawling monstrosity, he raised his primary weapon at waist height and stitched a burst of automatic fire into the skull to obliterate it.

"Stay!" he said conversationally, as the others joined him at his side.

"Well, would you fucking look at that," Smiffy spoke with an incredulous tone, "that is the worst fucking outfit I have *ever* seen."

Chuckles sounded among the four men as they finally took stock of what the nearly headless Lima had been wearing before he'd died and turned.

"I mean, come on," Mac said, picking up the thread, 'this wanker actually *chose* to wear that when he was alive."

The four men looked down, regarding a shiny shellsuit so offensive that none of them could make sense of the number of bright colours which adorned the body; it looked just as if he'd been wearing white, and had turned inside a paint shop and thrashed around until he was covered from head to toe.

"Reckon the guy who owns Campari is still alive?" Dezzy asked as they turned and began to walk back, reloading their weapons.

"If he is," Smiffy answered, "can we just pretend he's a zombie and slot him anyway?"

"My thanks, gentlemen," Palmer's voice cut over their chatter. They looked up to see the young captain in command of the armour approaching them.

"I did say we would see each other soon," Downes said, offering a hand for him to shake.

"You did," Palmer accepted, "but I didn't think it would be so soon, nor under such circumstances."

"True, Captain," Downes said, "very true. Have you contacted your base yet?"

Palmer's face dropped into annoyance and worry before he answered, nudging his head to one side and indicating that the SAS officer should follow him away for a private talk.

"No, they aren't responding to our calls. Do you think we can push through to retake the bridge?" he asked.

Downes thought, casting his mind back to the rotting, rolling hills of dead and writhing bodies.

"No, we have to find another way. I doubt your wagons would punch through and going on foot is suicide."

"Dammit," Palmer cursed, then turned as his name was called urgently from the open hatch of the Sultan behind him.

FOUR

Long before the German tanks had been mobilised and the combined UK special forces teams had arrived at their underground objective in London, an allied team had been covertly inserted onto British soil. They did so via the side door of a twin propeller plane, and the team of four dropped out at just under ten thousand feet to freefall, before opening their canopies to arrive quietly at the twin of the nuclear power station near the south coast.

As the three men and one woman of the *Forsvarets Spesialkommando*, or FSK, plummeted towards the green landscape to the north and east of London, one of them marvelled that they were being deployed at all. The Norwegian government still hadn't officially acknowledged the existence of their elite commandos, even though they had been undergoing intensive training ready to play their part for NATO should the Cold War gather any kind of intense heat. Now, instead of deploying in secret under cover of darkness to erode the infrastructure of the Soviet Union, they were heading down to secure a location for a team of American engineers to turn down the dial on the nuclear power plant.

The first parachute commando out of the door, eager to be the first pair of boots on the ground and prove that she was more capable than any man, levelled herself out and glanced at the altimeter on her left wrist as she reached terminal velocity. She knew the other three men of her team would be close behind her, but the low cloud cover prevented them from seeing their objective from height.

As Astrid Larsen fell, she adjusted her attitude to allow for her right hand to reach behind and pull the cord to release her parachute above the cloud cover so as not to issue a loud crack when the chute deployed at low altitude. Taking a breath and holding it, she steadied her torso against the violent change in direction as the air caught the canopy to snatch her vertically. As soon as she located the steering lines she heard a whistling, flapping noise and checked up again to ensure that her rig had deployed correctly, but her vision was drawn to a man-sized missile.

Her commander, Erik Nilson, last man out of the plane, flew past her out of control and left her with a snapshot of his hand pulling desperately on the reserve 'chute. Within a heartbeat he was gone, swallowed by the cloud layer sitting close to the ground, and another noise pulled her eyes back up. Spiralling and yelling in fear and frustration, another of her team fell at a far faster rate than her own descent, as he twisted inexorably, agonisingly, trying to release the partially-open canopy that dragged him down at a rate he couldn't hope to survive. He too disappeared into the clouds, and a second later she followed, pursing her lips against the sudden cool sting of the moisture.

Emerging through the layer herself, she took in the scene below, which set her jaw tight and forced her adrenaline levels higher still.

The compound, strongly fenced and very secure, as she

would expect with anything nuclear, had somehow been infected with the disease that threatened Europe and the wider world, and this had the unfortunate side effect of containing the enemy inside a confined area. Having inexplicably lost at least fifty percent of their strength in the drop, Astrid forced herself to concentrate and find a safe place to land. Hauling on the steering lines, she aimed for a single storey building and its flat roof, flaring the canopy with all of her strength at the last moment to try and arrest as much of her momentum as possible. Losing her footing on the loose tar and shingle, she scraped herself painfully along the roof until she could unfasten the straps of her rig and shrug out of it to unstrap the weapon from her chest. Astrid, like all of her team,

carried the same weapon as the UK special forces in the form of the MP5SD, the suppressed sub-machine gun, but unlike them, the Norwegians all carried the same HK P7 pistol with the fat cylinder protruding from the barrel, which she wore on her right thigh. Extending the parachute stock of the gun, she nestled it into her shoulder and took aim over the iron sights to the ground below.

She saw Nilsen, at least she assumed it was him as there was no canopy around the man, partly embedded in the soft grass, with limbs sticking out at horrendously unnatural angles. There was nothing she could do for him, as landing at terminal velocity wasn't much known for its survivability. Turning her head away from the stomach-churning sight of kneeling people tearing into her commander's body with teeth and nails, and thankful that she was too far away to hear the ripping and crunching noises she imagined, she looked towards the sounds of distress to her right.

Obscured by the angle of the building, she could see the upper body of another team member, the unfortunate one with the partially failed canopy deployment who'd come in too fast to control his landing. The man, Jonas, was caught up in an upright metal support by his snagged canopy. His right arm hung limply, and he cried out either in pain or fear, or both. Astrid didn't know what was beneath him, but she saw him struggling to free his pistol with his left hand and clamp the slide under his chin to charge the weapon. He achieved this on the second attempt and began to pour shots downwards towards an enemy Astrid couldn't see enough from her position. She stood to her full height to try and gain an advantage, but still could not sight his attackers. All too quickly, his magazine was expended, and he tucked the weapon under his arm as his rhythmic yells sounded short of breath. Performing a one-handed reload, he repeated the process to charge the weapon, but stopped to throw his head back and howl in pain. His whole body convulsed, and the firing resumed, but the yells stopped and his face flushed red. Finally locating Astrid in his vision, he shot her a look of panic, fixed her stare for a second, and turned the gun on himself.

Astrid watched him, her face a silent rictus of horror as the top of his skull burst to fountain blood and bone directly upwards before his limp, lifeless head and body slumped down. He twitched, shaking as though someone was trying to help him down from where he hung in the tangled lines, and the realisation hit her at the same time as his body was pulled down out of sight, that he was being consumed by ravenous teeth. Scrapes to her left made her drop to her right knee and raise the gun, with her left arm resting on her left knee, providing instant stability to the weapon. As soon as she had sighted down the length of the barrel, she immediately pointed the weapon up and relaxed.

Christian Berg, the only other surviving member of her team, had landed on his feet perfectly and jogged a handful of steps with the momentum to slow down as he stepped out of the rig he had unfastened on landing.

Under any other circumstance, such a stylish entrance would prompt bragging and laughter, but as the last man to land, he had seen the whole grim show unfolding. Unstrapping his own gun and extending the stock, he asked Astrid in their native Norwegian what she knew.

"The commander is dead," she reported, by pointing at the knot of kneeling figures who feasted on him, "and Jonas just put a bullet in his own brain."

"Bitten?" Berg asked.

"I didn't see, but I have to assume so. He was hung up in his lines," she said, pointing in the direction where his canopy flapped against the metal poles.

"Nilsen hit his canopy in freefall," Berg reported woodenly, "I didn't see it, but I heard it. Jonas must have been unable to recover."

Astrid pursed her lips in thought, sending up a brief prayer to the old gods for surviving what had become a catastrophic loss of life in seconds; fifty percent of their team dead from just their insertion was devastating.

"We still have the mission," she said, subtly reminding Berg that at less than two-thirds his size, she still outranked him. He nodded, stepping to the edge of the low building and bobbing his head fractionally as he scanned the ground, making a rough headcount of the visible zombies.

"Do you see any of the faster ones like in the intelligence report?" she asked his broad back.

"I can't be certain," he said cautiously, "but I would still prefer to stay up here until they are gone. Shall we?"

"What do you suggest?"

"We call them over," Berg said simply, "and shoot them."

Astrid shrugged, checked her watch and calculated the time left before the helicopter would be swooping in to drop off the engineers.

"You think it will work?" she asked.

Berg smiled, shrugging, and repeated a phrase that trans-lated into English as, *Birds fly not into our mouths ready roasted.*

Astrid understood; it was time to go to work.

It took them close to forty minutes to attract the attention of the majority of the zombies and draw them close enough to dispatch them with bullets to their heads. Those less interested in them had to be confronted at ground level and the pair moved close to each other, at one point ending up back to back when Berg was forced to resort to his secondary weapon, as it was quicker to draw and use the pistol than to reload the MP5. The air around them stank of cordite and their barrels ran hot as they expended most of their ammunition.

When they had finished, when no other enemies came for them and they were left dominant in the field, they finally had the time to attend to their fallen companions.

Or at least, attend to what was left of them.

Nilsen had somehow landed on his back and had been all but hollowed out. His face was gone, and his intestines had been spread over impossibly long distances as the zombies eating them had wandered towards the new sounds and dragged the glistening snakes with them. It was an ignoble and unworthy end to a respected, capable man, but the mission came first, and they managed to pick through his remains to recover the spare ammunition he carried. Both surviving members of the team were down to their last thirty rounds, as they had been forced to dispatch twice the number of enemy than would have been necessary, had they suffered no losses on the insertion. They found the body of Jonas, still partly suspended by his parachute, and tried not to look at the exposed bones of his legs where he had been chewed at like a hanging treat in a birdcage. Silently, his weapons and ammuni-tion were taken to replenish their expended rounds, and the pair entered the building with one of the swipe cards that the whole team carried.

The engineers arrived via helicopter less than an hour after they had secured the power station. Two men, tired and both wearing a few days' worth of stubble, followed their escort inside and went about their work in near silence, save for a few necessary words to each other. They finished quickly, far more quickly than the two surviving Norwegians had expected, and they packed up their gear to trudge exhaustedly back to the helicopter, which was sitting motionless on the hardstanding near the main entrance doors. Those doors were sealed behind them, and the helicopter's engines sparked into life to spin up the limp blades to a screaming whine.

Over that noise, Berg shouted a warning.

It wasn't any identifiable word, merely a panicked shout of rage and fear and alarm as he slammed his body into the path of the running shape rounding the corner of the building, like a professional sportsman checking an opponent. The combined impact of an inhumanly reckless run and the commando's large frame sent the five of them tumbling to the ground. Astrid rolled clear of the obstruction at the front of the melee and rose to her knees as she brought up her MP5 in one smooth movement, her right thumb pushing all the way down and flicking the fire selector through to automatic.

The fat barrel of the gun spat savagely, emptying the magazine into the rising creature as it leapt into the air to tower over her countryman. The end of the barrel tracked upwards with the movement as it rose, its chest rippling with the impacts of the bullets until finally the angle of the weapon elevated enough for the thudding noise to become hollower. The splintering, cracking sounds of the creature's skull coincided with the sudden limpness in the attack. At the peak of its ungainly leap, the wide, cloudy eyes over bared teeth went slack and it fell flat on top of Berg's broad back to drive the air out of him and the two engineers underneath. Its head flopped, pouring a mouthful of oily drool onto the rolled-up sleeve of one of them.

Silence reigned, broken only by Astrid sucking in a breath and dropping the spent magazine from her gun to click in a fresh one as she stood and kicked out at the torn and broken body to launch it off the living ones.

"Christian! Are you okay?" she asked in Norwegian in a tone bordering on panic, "Are you hurt?" she said insistently, speaking in English this time to all of them but still mostly concerned with her team mate.

"I am fine," Berg answered, his fingers going to the back of his head where it felt tender, to check his fingertips and find them sheened in the slightest trace of blood. He looked at the red smears on his skin, then at Astrid as they both registered a look of shock. Dropping her weapon to swing on the strap over her torso, she stepped forwards and pulled his head down to look for a wound. Berg said nothing. He wouldn't ask questions that he didn't want the answer to, nor would he offer empty reassurances to her.

"I can't see any broken skin," she said finally, feeling the relief in him as he sagged. He stood, looking at the two terri-fied Americans, who remained on the rough concrete bathed in the rotor wash of the helicopter spinning up above them.

"You?" he said to them, watching as they checked them-selves over and offered shocked reassurances that they were fine.

"I grazed my elbow," one of them said weakly, showing a patch of scraped and bleeding skin. He looked dismayed when the minor injury was summarily ignored, and they were bundled into the helicopter. The two Norwegians put on head-sets and listened to the pilot as the helicopter's engines dialled up their intensity, and they rose into the air to turn south and

out to sea. Feeling the chill of the speed and altitude, the engineer with the fresh cut to his elbow pulled the gore-soaked
sleeves of his shirt down and felt the cold of wet blood and
drool on the injury, rubbing tenderly at it as he felt a sudden
sting.

CHAPTER

FIVE

"Hold the line, boys!" Lieutenant Chris Lloyd called out to his marines. "Conserve your ammunition!"

He pressed his own cheek back into the stock of his L85, the newly-issued SA80 rifle, renamed and given an innocuous codename, as was usually the way with the British Army. It was typically ironic that the SA80, as in small arms for the 1980s, only just started to come into issue when the decade began to draw to a close. Lloyd had seen how the RMPs and some troopers looked with jealousy at the Marines' guns, when they were still being issued with equipment left over from the second world war, or the sixties and seventies.

That jealousy, as much as he understood it, given the futuristic bullpup design of the rifle, was misplaced, in his opinion. He, or at least his sergeant, the irascible Bill Hampton, ensured that the marines kept their weapons in pristine condition. It was easy, given the amount of time they were hurrying up and waiting, but it was also a sad necessity, because every speck of dust, every grain of sand and every wet leaf or glob of mud seemed magnetically attracted to the gun's working parts. That was a constant source of annoyance, especially knowing that the word was beginning to spread that the forces would be conducting build-up training for a sandy theatre of war very soon. No major prizes were issued for guessing where that would have been, but it seemed unlikely that they would be deploying anywhere soon.

A shriek to his front focused his mind as the fence before him bent nauseatingly inwards. This prompted a sharp thrust of the attached bayonet into the open mouth of the dripping wet teenager in a navy blazer and diagonally-striped tie, the entire scene eerily lit by the flames of the burning building growing larger off to his right.

At least the bloody spike doesn't malfunction, he thought to himself.

As another surge of bodies swept over the fallen schoolboy, Lloyd stepped back and fired a long burst of automatic 5.56 at head height and temporarily cleared a section five paces wide. Clicking on an empty chamber, he hit the release catch and missed as the empty magazine fell away, out of his fingertips. Ignoring the drop, he snatched a fresh magazine from the pouch of his webbing and slapped it home to rack the bolt and feed a fresh bullet into the chamber. Bringing the rifle back into his shoulder and nestling it in tight, he inadvertently caught the annoyingly sensitive magazine release catch again, and succeeded in firing only a single round before he clicked dry again.

"Fucking..." he swore as he turned the weapon to look for the fault. He saw it instantly as the profile of the weapon looked almost ridiculous without a magazine seated behind the trigger mechanism. He felt a thump on his shoulder and turned to see the troop medic firing his own weapon one-handed, as his left hand held out the dropped ammunition to his officer.

"Thanks," Lloyd shouted, not that he expected Sealey to hear or answer him. The man was working, as were all of his marines as they fought incessantly to prevent the impossible tide of dead rolling out of the water like waves of animated meat.

His men were fighting shoulder to shoulder with others. There were three men wearing scarlet berets, whose long self-loading rifles (SLRs) barked loud reports of the heavier 7.62 rounds over the sharp crack of their own lighter ammunition, to over-penetrate and sometimes take more than one Screecher out, as the heavy bullets ripped through the meat wall ahead of them. Add to that the rattling, staccato sounds coming from the Sterling sub machine guns fired by the troopers of the dismounted armour squadron, and the shrieking moans from their enemy, the noise was confusing, terrifying and deafening.

Antiquated as they were in Lloyd's mind, those submachine guns still killed zombies just as effectively as their new rifles.

He didn't know what was going on in the rear, nor could he hope to know that he and his men were wasting ammunition when they should just have been getting off the island by any means necessary.

———

"What the hell was that?" Denise Maxwell said in response to a muted scream from outside. She and her daughter were in the front room of the empty townhouse halfway up the hill which was being shared with the injured Graham Ashdown, her husband's second in command, and his wife and son too.

Another scream sounded, closer this time, and was deeper in tone than the first.

"Okay, something's definitely going on," she said as she rose to her feet, "other than whatever's happening down there, I mean," she explained, meaning the incessant small arms gunfire from below.

She stepped close to the door and pressed her ear to the

wood, holding her breath to try and hear more of whatever was beginning to unfold on the island, while the others in the room stayed quiet. Screaming and flailing her arms, Denise flew back away from the door to land half on an armchair covered in a hideously patterned coarse brown material.

The door banged again, desperate hammering making the two young children cry and huddle away from the door. Just before one of them voiced their fears, another noise added to the banging.

"Denise, are you there?" hissed a woman's voice, "let me in if you're there, *please!*"

Flying back to her feet, Denise flicked the lock over and pulled the door wide to scan left and right in the narrow street, before grabbing the woman by her clothing and pulling her inside unceremoniously. Dishevelled, red-faced and half out of breath, Kimberley Perkins spilled inside and for once didn't try to hide the scarring on the left side of her face.

The bumpy, mottled skin showed up a different colour from her flushed cheeks, but the situation outside was obviously more pressing than her insecurities.

"They're here," she said in a shaking voice through gasps of breath, "on the island. We need to go!"

The news left them shocked into silence. That silence seemed to anger Kimberley, and she turned to look for bolts on the door, only to make another desperate sound of exasperation as she found none.

Damn these country people and their unlocked doors, she cursed to herself, having to satisfy her need for security by killing the main light and flicking over the catch to make sure the feeble door was locked. In the gloom of the darkened interior she walked confidently towards Denise and grabbed her arm to shake her out of her shock.

"Denise, we have to get off the island now," she said to her as kindly as she could, but failing to hide the intensity and fear from her voice, "Where should we go?"

Denise's eyes met hers, but her mouth opened to emit nothing but silence. She opened and closed it twice, her look turning from dull shock to something leaning heavily towards debilitating fear, until she finally managed to speak.

"We," she cleared her throat, "we have to get my hu-"

Her eyes grew wider as she realised that her husband, Simon Maxwell, was still out on a mission.

"There's no time," Kimberley snapped, "we can't just wait to be rescued. Now, *how do we get off the island?*" she said, shaking Denise again.

"We need a vehicle," Ashdown said as he struggled to stand. His neck was still bandaged, and his left arm was in a sling after the near-miss escape from when half of a former Royal Military Policeman had dragged him from his moving vehicle and tried to eat him alive.

"We load up and get to the bridge, but there's a tank blocking it," he finished.

"Can't we tow it out of the way?" his wife asked as she clutched their son to her side.

"It's a tank. It weighs more than fifty tonnes," he said, but seeing that his words hadn't made themselves clear, he explained it simply, "there's no way in hell we can drag it clear."

"So?" Kimberley snapped, eager to speed up the process.

"The helicopters," Denise said, "Go up the hill and get on a helicopter."

She had started grabbing up her possessions, throwing items into a fabric shopping bag with round, wooden handles that clacked together in her hand.

"And after that, I have no idea," she finished.

"After that," Kimberley said, "is irrelevant unless we get the hell off this bloody island."

They moved, leaving via the back door to the house and filing along the cobbled rear path past the wall of dark brick. Kimberley walked at the front, the two women with their children in the middle and the slow-moving but armed Graham Ashdown at the rear.

Kimberley stopped at the wooden gate, secured with a twisted loop of wire hung loosely over the post which caught the gate, and it perplexed her momentarily until she saw it and pushed it upwards to free their escape route. Pausing to look back at the small flock she was leading, her eyes caught a glint of dull reflection. Turning towards it, she took in the shape of the short wooden handle and the wedge-shaped head of the small splitting axe stuck into a piece of wood. It had obviously been recently used, given the bright slices of fresh wood on the half-covered pile, and she reached out to snatch it up on impulse.

The worn curvature of the handle felt somehow reassuring in her grip, but not as reassuring as the weight of the head when it came loose from the grasp of the wet wood it was partly buried in. She hefted it once, feeling the weight and the way it moved in her hand, and she turned her eyes back to the darkening streets to lead her people uphill towards what she hoped was safety.

———

"Behind!" Marine Sealey screamed, repeating the warning and simultaneously turning away from the bending fences to advance three paces and drop to one knee. He pressed his eye into the scope and began squeezing off disciplined rounds in ones and twos, forcing Lieutenant Lloyd to realise the peril he and his men were in. He looked back, seeing a loose formation of uniformed men and civilians shambling towards their undefended rear.

Undefended, at least, until their medic turned to pick up the magazine for his weapon that he had dropped much in the same way as his Lieutenant had. He had recognised the jerky movement of the ex-people behind him instantly and shouted the warning as he began to pour careful fire into heads.

They were so close that the skulls filled his scope, forcing him to take his eye away after he had expended half of the magazine to locate the next closest attacker and drill a round through their head. The detail in the scope showed him flashes, almost like mental Polaroid pictures, of things he didn't want to remember.

An eye plastered shut with thick blood pouring downwards from a deep gash to a scalp. A nose bitten clean off, exposing the two gaping holes of nostrils as though the flesh hadn't been completed over the skull. A throat torn clean out, showing a bloody network of tubes and sinew underneath a mouth that screeched but emitted no sound.

Standing tall, leaning into his weapon and bawling for his men to turn around and fight off the rear assault, he swallowed his fear and resolved to fight harder than he had before. More weapons joined that fight and just as terrifyingly sudden as that attack had begun, it faded further away, and allowed them to take more carefully aimed shots at heads not so disturbingly close.

Renewed shouts of alarm sounded from behind them and Lieutenant Lloyd turned to see the harsh consequences of taking away half of their guns for a few precious moments. The fences and long lines of cruel barbed wire were pushed inwards and worryingly close to what must be their breaking point, where they threatened to give way at any moment under the crushing weight of Screechers crawling out of the water to flood his small force.

Lloyd faced a choice, an imminent and desperately important choice, and he had only a few precious seconds to make it before his inaction threatened the lives of everyone. He looked once back up the hill, then back to where the sea was spewing undead horrors onto their inadequate defences, and he made his decision.

"Fall back! Fall back!" he bawled at the rag-tag collection of military police, yeomanry and marines. "On me!"

With that last command, he ran out ahead of the men and steadied his footing before thrusting the fixed bayonet into the eye of a woman he half recognised from the island. He thought nothing of that act; he couldn't afford the time or the distraction caused by emotions or sentimentality. Without looking to see if the men behind were following him, he pressed on ahead through the streets with his rifle up in a fast-forward, reckless approximation of the FIBUA course, the fighting in built-up areas training he had led his men through before their most recent tour in Northern Ireland. Had the instructors seen his insane dash into danger, he would have instantly failed the course, but they weren't fighting snipers and bombers now. They were fighting a new infantry that didn't use weapons, didn't lure them out of their protective vehicles to detonate home-made explosives packed into ice cream tubs. They merely swarmed over them in great numbers without feeling pain or holding any regard for anything but a bullet or a bayonet to the brain.

He moved fast, his nerve finally breaking and forcing him to glance behind to see a tight knot of soldiers moving in support. He saw two scarlet berets among the bare heads, and the dark green headgear of his men, and he guessed that he must have absorbed some of the others with him. The cacophony surrounding him made it difficult to discern between the different reports, but he was certain that he could hear three distinctly different weapon reports coming from the loose formation of men catching him up amidst the gunfire and the screams and the now raging crackling of the burning buildings nearer the road bridge.

"Where are we going, Sir?" one of the army men asked him.

"Up," he answered, racking the bolt to seat another bullet, ready to fire in his rifle after reloading. "Bring as many people as we can along the way, but the island is lost."

To the credit of each man there, none of them showed anything but a grim and determined resolve to survive. They were cut off, the enemy was among them, and they had to fight.

CHAPTER

SIX

"Send," Palmer snapped into the radio handset, then frowned as he listened to the response. Johnson watched his face, not liking what he saw, and glanced to the only other man present who was privy to the information.

Corporal Daniels, normally a steady man, looked ashen. His mouth opened slightly, his eyes went vacant and he trembled. Johnson looked back to the Captain.

"Understood," he said simply in a voice that sounded hollow and final, "good luck. Out."

He handed the handset back to Daniels, having to nudge the man in the shoulder with it to bring him back to his senses and take the offered equipment.

"SSM, the island is…" he paused, swallowing, "the island is cut off. There was a shore bombardment from the navy, and unfortunately it brought the bridge down with the loss of one of our MBTs."

Johnson slumped back in the too-small chair and looked aghast. The loss of the main battle tank was a huge blow, but the bridge being brought down was their worst-case scenario. They couldn't fight their way back home, nor could their reinforcements come to their aid; any vehicle left on the island was staying there.

"It gets worse, I'm afraid," Palmer said as he rubbed his face, fingers scratching on the fair stubble of his cheeks. "The virus is loose there. There's an outbreak, and I fear that very few of them are going to make it out."

That news, and the sinking realisation with it, dropped Johnson's heart straight down through his guts. For some bizarre reason he couldn't fathom, his thoughts went to the attractive woman who inexplicably wanted to get to know him. These thoughts came to him in a flash, much faster than time passed, as though the feelings and thoughts all arrived at once and were decoded instantly in his mind. He guessed she would never get the chance to know him now, and he regretted his guarded responses to her questions all those hours ago when they had enjoyed a companionable drink with Maxwell and his wife.

Maxwell, he thought selfishly as he tried to find a way to tell him, *Shit, Denise! The kids!*

Palmer seemed to read his thoughts and held up a hand to stop the question before it was formed in Johnson's mouth.

"Yes, most of the men have people there, have *family*, myself included…" he said, making Johnson feel a small stab of regret for the junior Lieutenant, not out of sadness for losing the man, but for the pain that loss would bring his older brother. Even more wretchedly, he realised that sadness wasn't for any regretful loss of life, but for the fact that it would make their officer less efficient. He let the silence hang heavy for a moment before the Squadron Sergeant Major cleared his throat and asked a simple question.

"What are our orders, Sir?"

Palmer turned slowly to regard him, his face morphing out of stunned sorrow and back into something infinitely more tempered by professionalism, and his words sounded confident and resolved.

"Ammo count, half of the guns cleaned at once," he said, dishing out administrative tasks that levelled the men with familiar activity, "Assault Troop to recce south for high ground and try and observe the island," he said, and then remembered that Assault Troop was down to a single vehicle and a scattering of men among the other vehicles. "Cancel that. Send a pair of Foxes."

Johnson nodded, then rose to pull himself out of the open hatch above. He was on the verge of reminding the Captain that they only had one single Spartan of Assault Troop left, and no wagon ever rolled on its own, but the man had evidently recalled the facts and changed the order. The only foreseeable problem with the amended orders was a mechanical one; the Fox, as well armed as it was, performed like it was made of chocolate when asked to go off-road with any meaning.

He gave his orders to Strauss, one of the few men without family locally, and hence unburdened by the weight of the news Johnson was forced to keep to himself for the time being. He gave the orders, mixed with part of the information, that the bridge was down, and sent the two crews off to find the high cliffs overlooking the rock that used to be their temporary home.

As he walked back towards the command vehicle, the tall man wearing black clothing and dripping in non-standard weaponry cut across his path.

"Sarn't Major," he greeted him.

"Sir," Johnson answered.

"I wonder if you've had any joy contacting your base?"

Johnson looked over both shoulders and lifted his chin in the direction of the Sultan. The SAS men had only a personal radio set which required complex setting up, differing lengths of antennae, the blood of a unicorn and a bucket brimming with good luck to make it work sometimes, whereas their command vehicle had three sets permanently working.

"Best you come and speak to the Captain, Sir," he said ominously.

Downes listened to Palmer's report wearing a blank look. His bright eyes oozed alertness, but his expression and features remained stock-still and emotionless.

"You still have RN aircraft there?" he asked, meaning the navy helicopters, one of which had only recently removed their precious cargo and half of the special forces soldiers.

"Unable to raise them," Palmer said, "one would hope they are evacuating personnel…"

"Indeed," Downes responded before changing the subject, "what's your redundancy?"

Palmer looked shocked, mainly because he hadn't considered abandoning the island and resorting to occupying a back-up location, at least not without proof that the island was beyond their help. His lack of answer gave Downes the information regardless.

"In the absence of orders from command and any viable way to assist anyone left at base, you will need to consolidate," Downes said. "I would suggest that we form up in sight of the base and prepare to receive any additional personnel via helicopter, but after that it is our duty to remain operational."

Palmer viewed him as coolly as he could, fighting the urge to snap at the senior officer out of fear and frustration. He kept his head level and his eyes fixed when he answered.

"Are you assuming control of the men, Sir?" he asked formally, leaving a tense and awkward silence.

"No, Captain," Downes said with a small smile intended to appease the younger man, "I am not. Merely making a suggestion."

"Very well," Palmer said, returning the smile to show that

his hostility was fleeting, "I've deployed two wagons to get sight of the island, and we will wait for their report. Anything else you need, Sir?"

"No, Captain, just shout us if you need us."

With that, Downes climbed up and out of the Sultan awkwardly, showing them that he was not used to travelling in an armoured squadron. Palmer turned back to Daniels as soon as the

sound of his boots hitting the rocky ground outside floated in through the open hatch.

"Corporal, keep trying the island. Use the RN and marine frequencies too if you can," he said, watching as Daniels snatched up a piece of paper that had numbers scribbled in pencil on it from where he had wedged it beside his radios, "and let me know as soon as One Troop provide a report."

———

"Well?" Mac asked Downes as he ducked back inside the open rear door of the Saxon.

"Well, their base is cut off, looks like the navy tried to help and accidentally blew the bridge," he waited as the snorts of derision rippled around his three men, "and they can't raise anyone on comms to see if they are flying them out, because there's an outbreak on the island. Fuck knows where this is going."

He let them assimilate the new information in their own time, copying their actions of refilling spent magazines from the big bag of bullets laid out between them. That bag, as heavy as it must have been, had been strapped to Mac's back the entire time they had been deployed, as though it weighed nothing.

"And us?" Dez asked as he thumbed bullets into the metal and compressed the spring.

"Nothing from central command yet, they're still trying, and unless we use their Sultan to re-bro us, then I doubt we'll have much luck ourselves," Downes answered, meaning the Yeomanry's ability to re-broadcast the communications from their man-portable radios through the command vehicle and increase the reliability ten-fold.

"Are they just not getting through," Mac asked in his characteristically grim tone, "or are they not answering us?"

"I don't know," Downes said pensively, "but I don't like it."

———

The Bell helicopter carrying the two engineers and the two surviving Norwegians flared in to scrape its skids on the deck of the dull grey American vessel, the USS Mearle, beside the taller, bulbous airframe of a Royal Navy Sea King. Deck crew wearing their different coloured helmets ran low towards them and helped the four passengers down.

"Captain wants to see you two," shouted one man, pointing behind himself at a sealed doorway leading inside. Astrid glanced up at Berg's face, seeing nothing betrayed in his stony expression. Technically they didn't fall under anyone's command, but with the situation as it was, any senior leadership still active under the NATO banner took authority of troops they found stranded or abandoned with them. The two Norwegians walked towards the doorway and into the gloomy interior without looking back to the engineers, one of whom was growing pale and had broken out in a sweat.

The ship was a hive of well-run efficiency, with people teeming the decks and everyone working like ants to play their own small part in keeping the destroyer operating at maximum capacity. The arrival of two civilian nuclear engineers on a non-nuclear warship was of such little importance that nobody noticed them. Nobody noticed the pale man stagger slightly as his feet hit the deck, not even his fellow engineer, and his arrival went totally undetected.

He followed the lead, winding his way across the flat top of the landing space, and bounced heavily off the doorway to crash bodily into the bulkhead inside.

"Hey, buddy," said a sailor approaching them, "you okay, man?"

"Yeah," he gasped as he tried to stand and smile to show he was fine, "just feeling a little queasy, you know?"

"Ah," the sailor responded with a grin, "you'll get your sea-legs soon, don't sweat it."

The engineer smiled weakly again, stood upright, then rolled his eyes back into his head and pitched backwards to slam unconscious into the deck.

————

"Okay, how long has he been out?" asked the diminutive doctor as he strode into the treatment bay in the ship's medical department.

"Only a few minutes," said the sailor who had bodily carried him there to save time, "reckons he was seasick or something."

The doctor placed one hand on the engineer's forehead and frowned.

"Seasickness doesn't usually cause a fever, sailor," he said, then announced more loudly to his medically personnel, "I need IV fluids and get these clothes cut off. We can't rule out infection."

"Infection?" the sailor asked, wearing a suddenly worried look on his young face and taking an involuntary step backwards.

"The first sign of this virus," the doctor explained as he was helping to strip the man, "is a raised temperature. After that it varies, depending on the severity of the injury. Get me a vitals monitor on, somebody?" he called out to the room.

The sailor carried on backing away, mumbling something about returning to his duty, and left the engineer to have his clothes cut away from his body. Heavy shears chomped at the thick material covering his legs to reveal pale flesh. The doctor had recognised his pallor and ordered the fluids as a first measure to prevent the man going into shock. Checking every part of his

body meticulously, the only break in the man's skin was in the form of a small graze at his elbow. The injury was less than superficial, but the swollen, angry red skin around it screamed infection. He checked the graze closely, unable to find anything resembling a bite mark, and chewed his lip in thought.

"Okay, I need two hundred ccs of IV antibiotics, flush it through with saline and keep the fluids going. This man has a severe infection, but it doesn't appear to be *that* infection," he announced as he stepped back and peeled off his surgical gloves. He left the treatment room to return to his other patients, feeling satisfied that he had averted disaster for the time being.

The engineer, unconscious and having already spoken his last words, burned up from the inside. The combined spittle and blood from the last zombie Astrid had dispatched after Christian Berg had driven them all to the ground had soaked his shirtsleeve and leaked into the open cut on his arm and infected him. The severity of the infection was lessened by the means, but the end result was just as inexorable as if his throat had been bitten out.

The doctor had been called back in and had ordered an ice bath to be used to try and break the fever and prevent damage to the brain. No amount of medication or any other intervention had brought the man's temperature down, and his convulsions raged intensely for half a minute until he went suddenly

still. Paddles were charged as the man was hauled unceremoniously out of the ice bath and dried off desperately, but they
were too late to save his life.

"Time of death," the doctor said, glancing up at the clock
on the bulkhead, "eighteen-thirty-two. Someone find out who
he was, and I'll inform the Captain."

SEVEN

"Welcome aboard the Mearle," announced the tall, almost gangly man who rose from his command chair on the bridge. The two FSK commandos stood rigid for a moment, seemingly all that would pass for a salute to the American, and he shrugged as if to convey that he didn't expect anything more. His gaze lingered on Astrid for a half-second longer than he had regarded Berg.

"I'm Captain Alder, this is Commander Briggs from the British Navy," he said, indicating another tall, thin man who had risen and now offered a hand to them.

"*Royal* Navy," he corrected the American, who shrugged again and allowed one corner of his mouth to lift in a small smirk.

"Your report?" Alder asked them as he retook his seat. Berg glanced at Larsen, who raised her eyebrows slightly before responding.

"Chto vy dumayeshe?" Astrid muttered to Berg quietly in informal Russian, as they often did when they didn't want to be understood by others.

Berg answered her question of, 'What do you think?' with a

shrug of his own, meaning that he saw no reason to withhold anything.

"What do you know of our mission?" she asked, ever careful and secretive.

"Assume I know everything up to you getting there," Alder responded in a tone that indicated he had no time left for need-to-know matters. Astrid kept her face neutral as she cursed the arrogance of the man inside the safety of her own thoughts.

"We suffered fifty percent fatalities during insertion," she began in deadpan but perfect English, "we cleared the objective and protected the engineers as they shut down the plant. We were extracted."

Captain Alder, clearly annoyed at the brevity of the report, needled her with his next question.

"Too many of the infected there for you?"

"No," she snapped back, a little too quickly and forcefully and betraying her raw nerves about it, "there was a parachute malfunction which caused our commander to land at terminal velocity. On his way in he caught the rig of our other man and tangled him up. He survived the landing but was caught up. They started eating his legs, so he shot himself in the head."

Alder took his turn to keep a neutral face and dropped the goading in an instant.

"I'm sorry to hear that. Well done on completing the mission. Get some food and rack time and we'll see about getting you home, but we've got more than enough to be getting on with here. Dismissed."

Both commandos stiffened again and turned away, seeing the sympathetically smiling face of Commander Briggs. He finished polishing the lenses of his glasses on the tail of his black uniform tie and gestured for them to follow him out of the bridge.

"We are a little overcrowded here, as is everyone in the joint fleet, I should imagine. There's food being served in the galley and I'm sure you'll be able to find somewhere suitable to rest your heads for a while if you wish," he said almost apologetically as though he was unable to be as gracious a host as he could be.

"You are English, so why are you here?" Berg asked in an enquiring tone so direct that it bordered on rude.

"I was attached as an aide between Her Majesty's forces and our American allies," Briggs answered blankly, as though he wanted to say more but was simply too well-mannered and polite to voice his opinion. They followed him in silence until he had shown them the head, galley and an area that was used for makeshift beds which were little more than a thin mattress and some stiff blankets. They still carried their weapons, which under normal circumstances would have raised eyebrows or even attracted challenges, but it seemed that every third person they saw had a sidearm on their belts or even carried long guns. They ate, at least they put some stodgy form of food inside their bodies out of nothing more than an ingrained need to stay fully effective, and then they found a quiet corner to clean their weapons.

Which they had no idea they would need far sooner than expected.

———

The engineer, pale and naked on a metal gurney in the medical, opened his eyes. They weren't the eyes he had previously seen through, in fact he could barely see a thing, not that he could comprehend anything he saw through them anyway. The eyes were milky orbs, his skin remained deathly pale and his right hand twitched in unison with his fluttering eyelids.

The two medical orderlies, their backs turned to him as they chatted inanely about an upcoming baseball game, as though the world weren't burning all around them, didn't notice the small movements of what they thought was a dead body behind them.

The engineer sat up slowly, demonstrating a core strength that he did not know he'd possessed when his actions were cognitive, then he bent at the waist and rose silently, fixing his half-blind gaze on the backs of the two young sailors who were still talking without a care in the world. Swinging his right leg off the cold gurney and slapping it gently onto the cold deck, he followed it with his other leg as his eyes stayed glued to the source of the sound. As his second foot slapped down, the slight noise made the hairs on the back of one orderly prickle, and he turned to see the dead body standing upright and staring straight at him.

He turned back, frowning, and looked at his friend, before opening his eyes wide in terror as his head whipped back to the standing corpse.

Too late, he found himself face to face with the body, which was a head taller than he was. Cold hands clamped either side of his face as the sharp fingernails dug painfully into the thin flesh over his skull, but no scream came from him as the open mouth of the zombie clamped hard onto his own and bit hard to tear his lips and the tip of his tongue away in one savage rip. The zombie rocked, staggered one pace to its right, then turned to mindlessly view the source of disruption. Dropping the shaking, gargling mess of the young man it had already infected, the thing that used to be an engineer turned and cocked its head slightly at the other sailor, who was nursing a hand with broken bones after throwing a pointless right hook into the side of its head. Stepping backwards and babbling incoherently, his shoulders clattered into a wall cupboard and bounced him back slightly.

Directly into the jaws of the naked man, who bit into the right side of his neck so hard that the last sound he heard was a crunching noise followed by a squelch. Hot blood ran down his upper body and he blacked out, never to wake again. Not alive, at least.

The second sailor's body hit the deck and knocked down a tray of instruments, making a harsh rattle of metal echo into the gangway outside the sealed door. The falling instrument tray made an IV stand teeter, before finally toppling over to bang loudly against a metal surface just as two other sailors were walking past.

The two men froze, looking at each other in silent question. One of them rapped his knuckles against the metal door and called out, asking if everything was okay in there. The only response was a strangled, screeching cry from inside, a cry that the two sailors had not heard before and did not have a hope of comprehending, and they threw open the door to offer assistance.

———

"What do you think we will do next?" Berg asked Astrid quietly in their native language as they cleaned their weapons.

"Probably go home and wait years for another mission," she replied sullenly, before she remembered that she should act the part of the senior commando, even if there were only two of them left of their unit.

"Will they try to reclaim the countries lost to the disease?" he asked almost rhetorically, "or just seal them off and let it die out?"

"Will it die out?" she asked, perplexed that the concept of a virus burning itself out of a host was a possibility.

Berg shrugged.

"Who knows? Some scientists at home think that the infected hosts will all eventually die out."

Astrid stopped cleaning her MP5 as she considered what he had said. The theory was feasible, she had to admit, as the ones she had seen all smelt like they were rotting. She had to accept that if the infected weren't preserved, then they would eventually decompose enough to not pose a threat to the living.

Almost simultaneously, the two FSK commandos finished reassembling their clean weapons and clicked fresh magazines into place. Weapon discipline made them not chamber a round, as the effects of a negligent discharge inside a small metal box weren't worth the risk, and both drew their pistols to clean them just as an alarm sounded. The two looked at each other, neither willing to take the risk that it was just a drill or a false alarm, and both stood to ready themselves for yet another fight.

———

By the time the engineer had infected and killed four of the sailors, it had stumbled out of the open doorway, still naked except for a sheet of red blood down its front from the dark mouth that chewed at an unrecognisable chunk of gristly flesh hanging past the bloody chin. It paused in the empty gangway, head swinging left and right as it searched for the next sound to entice it onwards. A shout from the right made it stagger off in that direction, just as the first medical orderly, with a ragged chunk torn from his neck, rose to his feet, opened his own sightless eyes, and staggered off after his killer.

The infection spread rapidly, as each open compartment was packed with people who had no means of escaping a threat they weren't prepared for. The two zombies ravaged the human contents of three compartments, killing everyone inside without mercy or thought. Sailors beat at them with fists, with furniture, but the confines of the ship's interior were too cramped, and nobody brought a weapon to bear. By the time the death toll had reached double figures, the three bodies from the medical bay had risen and wandered off in another direction, and so the disease spread undetected and rapidly below decks.

By the time the first shot fired blew the entire right side of the engineer's face away, there were close to twenty animated corpses roaming the lower decks, tearing flesh with nails and teeth. The engineer slumped forwards as though the power had been cut to his body, but stepping awkwardly over his prone body came more monsters just as eager to rip away skin and disembowel anything not already dead. The rest of the magazine was expended in rapid fire, but the shots were wasted into the chest cavity of the medical orderly, who fell upon the sailor with the gun, as his teeth found the exposed skin above the collar of his uniform.

He died, gargling and spasming uncontrollably as his finger pulled repeatedly on the trigger to punctuate the sounds of his violent death with the sound of the gun clicking dry.

———

"Something is definitely not right," Astrid told her tall companion. In answer, Berg simply readied his MP5 and pointed it away from them as he chambered a round to make the gun ready. She copied his actions and the two settled into a ready crouch to make their way back towards sunlight, as though the outside offered any more protection than the tight corridors below decks.

They stalked onwards, the harsh sound of the insistent, repetitive klaxon drowning out their words and forcing them to communicate on a level that only highly-trained soldiers could manage. With looks and nods they cleared the corners and secured doors so as not to leave any surprises behind themselves. As they climbed the ladder to the next deck they encountered people moving; running in panic, and amidst the chaos one or two voices rose to force order on the sailors.

Lowering their weapons and keeping their eyes down, the two Norwegians pushed their way through the crowds, hearing snippets of conversation and questions. Wearing plain clothing with no insignia or rank helped, as they were assumed to be outside of any military hierarchy. As the mass of people dissipated, they rounded another corner and came face to face with two men dressed similarly. Both were fiercely bearded, all seemed to recognise the elite status of the others as one glance at their weaponry told them that they were on a similar level.

"Larsen and Berg. FSK," Astrid said over the sound of the alarm.

"Bufford. SBS," said the man at the lead, before nodding over his shoulder and introducing the other man as Owens.

"What's happening?" she said to him.

"I overheard someone saying there was an outbreak below decks. It's probably spreading fast on ship. The quicker they die the quicker they turn," he added, making Larsen frown.

"You've seen it?" she asked.

"Not up close," he replied, "and I don't fucking want to either."

"Agreed. So how do we get off the ship?"

"Two of my boys are watching our helicopter. We've come back for the pilots," Bufford answered.

Astrid glanced at Berg, who simply nodded once.

"Do you have room for two more?" she asked.

The leader of the SBS team, having trained extensively in Norway with the Royal Marines before joining special forces, knew of the reputation of the FSK and agreed without hesitation. Another two well-handled MP5s supporting his team was not an asset to be ignored, in his opinion.

"Let's go then," he said and led the way.

CHAPTER

EIGHT

Lieutenant Commander Murray's co-pilot and loadmaster fell without even having a chance to put up a fight. The three of them were alone in a small compartment, occupying three of the four bunks, with the vacant mattress becoming home to their flight helmets and the loadmaster's rig. The door had been left open as they were waiting for orders, and they were as unaware of the drama unfolding on land as they were the lethal outbreak beneath their feet.

A knot of four men, all in US navy uniforms and all soaked in blood, burst into the open cabin and tore into the co-pilot before he knew what was happening. Only Murray, who was pulling up the top half of his all-in-one flight suit, was spared as he had yet to unlock the door to the head. They, or at least Murray, had lucked out as very few cabins had a bathroom even close to them, let alone inside, and only their supposed temporary stay had granted them a cabin near to the flight deck at the stern.

Now, with four strangers and two former friends banging and clawing at the door, he sat back down and waited for inspiration. Or death, whichever came first.

Bufford led his now four-man, or three men and one woman, team through the deck with speed and purpose as the klaxon stopped howling over the speakers. His other two men had been sent topside to make their way to the stern and the waiting Sea King. Their drills were slick, having all learned from the same advanced rule book, and he was grateful of the additional firepower after less than a minute, when one of the faster ones dressed as a cook but looking more like a butcher rocketed around a corner at a full sprint and cannoned off the bulkhead to sprawl on the deck ten paces from them. Instantly, he and Owens dropped to one knee and opened fire with single, controlled shots, just as the tall Norwegian stood over them and added a burst of

fire from his own weapon to ensure that the thing never got back to its feet. As they stood, Bufford looked behind to see the woman, Larsen, also rising up from her knee, as she had instantly turned to protect their rear. Satisfied that four was definitely better than two, they pushed on.

Glancing at a scribbled note in pen written on his left wrist in the gap between sleeve and glove, he checked the cabin designations to look for the flight crew.

He didn't know why he had done that, but something deep inside him said that he needed to be aware of them in case they had to leave in a hurry. He doubted he would have been so cautious on a Royal Navy vessel, but being away from Her Majesty's Forces' hospitality set him on edge.

"Four more, left side," he called out for the others to hear. No sooner had he said that, than the sounds of shrieking and banging echoed down the tight gangway to his ears, and he knew with total certainty that it was coming from the fourth cabin ahead on his left. Stalking as silently as he could, he held up one hand and sensed the others stack up behind him until a hand rested gently on one shoulder. He held up three fingers for them to see, folded one down, then gripped his weapon again and swung into the doorway to duck low. Owens came in behind him, weapon up high at shoulder height, and immediately the rounds spat from their guns to drill into the backs of skulls as six of them fought for space at the front of an interior door. Berg stepped inside to lean his head and shoulders through the door to take out one of them, before a thudding stream of automatic fire sounded in the corridor. Berg ducked back out, doubling the fire out there, but the two SBS men had to trust them and remain focused on removing the threats inside the small compartment.

As the last body, wearing the flying uniform of a Royal Navy officer, fell to the deck, the sounds of gunfire outside were replaced by metallic scrapes and clicks of guns being reloaded.

"We're clear," announced Bufford in a low voice.

"Clear here also," responded the woman's voice from behind him.

Bufford carefully stepped forward, firing one more single shot into the skull of a sailor who still twitched, and raised his gun again as another sound startled him. It was the sound of the door being pushed open and hitting the knee of a body, preventing it from opening more than a few inches, and the movement of his gun was met with a sudden cry of, "Don't shoot!"

"You the pilot?" Bufford asked as he lowered the gun all the way.

"What's bloody well left of him, yes," Murray spat back angrily as he shoved the door hard to make a big enough gap to squeeze out of. As he emerged, one shoulder of his dark suit seemed almost black in the unnatural light.

"Which one of you damned fools shot me?" he snarled through gritted teeth as the injured arm hung uselessly to drip fresh, bright red blood onto the corpses.

"Oh, for fuck's sake…" Bufford muttered before raising his voice, "either of you two medics?"

"I am," came Larsen's reply as she stepped carefully over the broken bodies and visually assessed the pilot.

"Sit down, take this off, please," she said as she slung her weapon and reached into a pouch to retrieve a package that she tore open with her teeth. She wiped the fresh blood away from the wound high up on Murray's right arm and pulled him around roughly to check for further injuries. Murray protested, issuing a few choice words in a hissed voice.

"Seems to be a flesh wound only," Larsen said, uncoiling the clotting bandage and wrapping it tightly around the injured body part, despite the pained noises coming from her patient.

"We are good to go," she said, the words sounding only slightly awkward in her mouth.

"Can you still fly?" Bufford asked intensely. Murray seemed to consider the question seriously, as though the concept of him flying with a bullet wound in his arm was even a possibility, and he flexed his bloody hand a few times as he rolled his shoulder with a wince.

"Not very far, but yes," he said quietly.

"Good. Can we get the fuck out of here then?" Owens said from the doorway, where he had joined Berg in protecting their exit.

With the same formation of the two SBS men in the lead and the two FSK commandos at the rear, they had Murray protected in the middle and holding a semi-automatic pistol taken from the holster of one of his besiegers. They moved more cautiously, more slowly as the injured Murray would not have been able to keep pace with their drills, even if one of them hadn't accidentally shot him with near catastrophic results. Gunfire rattled dully from the lower decks, muted by layers of metal which prevented the shrieks of attacking zombies from being clearly heard. The resulting cacophony was more of a white noise than any discernible sounds; more the *absence* of silence, or at least the absence of the normal sounds expected in that environment, that became deafening.

Corridor after corridor, ladder after ladder, zombie after zombie they moved onwards. They fought every step of the way, senses so heightened that their breath came in rapid gasps, and they cuffed at the sweat running into their eyes in the unnatural environment of heat and thick air that seemed to contain less oxygen than it should. The desire, the pathological *need* to get outside overtook them and heightened their stress levels immeasurably.

Eventually, to their great relief, they broke out into the afternoon sunlight and set foot onto the flat helicopter deck. Immediately the two pairs fanned out left and right to clear the wandering bodies in their path. The last few, too consumed with devouring a kill, didn't even turn around to face the new threat as they gorged on the fallen body they obscured from sight.

"No," Bufford said aloud, "oh fuck, *no!*" and ran forward towards the last few zombies.

"Buffs, wait," Owens growled before following, as he knew he would be ignored.

Bufford ran forwards, taking shots at the bloody beasts as he went, until his magazine ran dry. Reaching the supine body the zombies were gorging themselves on, he let the gun drop on its sling and reached for his right hip behind the pistol to draw his polished pioneer's axe. The final zombie, tall and broad and dressed in black with a beard as wild and unruly as Bufford's, rose up to stand over him and bear its teeth.

The axe swung downwards savagely, making the sickening crunch of bone and brain echo across the deck as it crumpled under the blow to land hard on the deck. Placing one boot on the shoulder of what had previously been his team mate, he pulled the axe clear and looked down at the second man he had personally sent to secure the area.

"Buffs," Owens said, placing a hand gently on his friend's shoulder but keeping a very wary eye on the hand holding the gore-smeared axe, "it's okay, mate. They're gone now…"

Owens trailed off as he looked down at the last member of the team. The two Norwegian commandos approached and glanced down at the two dead soldiers, both face-value carbon copies of the men they had joined forces with, from their weaponry down to their beards.

"Let's get the fuck out of here, then," Bufford said in a dead tone as he stripped the spare ammunition from his former team mates; acting as though he had washed away the loss and guilt but knowing that he was merely ignoring it for the time being.

Bypassing almost all of the checks required by the manual to safely get a Sea King helicopter into the air, they did the equivalent of jumping in a car and driving off without even adjusting the driving seat.

———

"Mayday, mayday, mayday," Captain Alder barked into the radio handset as his bridge crew were breaking out weapons from the lockers in the bulkheads, "USS Mearle reporting an outbreak. Repeat, we have infected onboard and require immediate assistan…" he flinched and dropped the mic as he fumbled for the pistol on his belt. The noise that had made him react was the double-assault of a body slamming heavily into the watertight door and the muted screeching noises that seemed to come from everywhere.

His hand shook, the barrel of the gun wavering as it pointed towards the sealed door, until good sense took over once more and he returned to the radio.

"Mayday, mayday, mayday, this is the USS Mearle reporting an outbreak. Requesting immediate assistance…"

The fleet flagship, and enormous floating city that housed the Admiral, was a polar opposite of the situation aboard the beleaguered destroyer. The Admiral, still and calm despite his mind screaming at the distress call playing over the loud-speaker, stood and smoothed down his uniform.

"Sailor, cut that," he said, meaning that he didn't want the transmission playing out loud any longer. There was nothing he could do to help those brave souls, but he knew that he had a duty to the world to make sure that the infection did not spread. That meant that the weight of the decision he was about to make and the consequences of the order he was ready to give rested squarely on his shoulders.

"Helmsman, take us out," he ordered, hearing the appropriate response and walking to a workstation covered in switches and dials. Picking up the satellite telephone used for communications which they couldn't afford to be overheard, he contacted the captain of the submarine silently slinking along in the depths like a shark. He gave his orders quietly, calmly, waited for the acknowledgement and ended the call.

He immediately placed another call, this time far to the west, and gave his recommendation.

"Understood, Admiral," came the reply from Washington, "initiate purge and quarantine. God Speed."

The Admiral returned to his chair and sat.

Lord, forgive me for what I have to do, he thought as he kept his face expressionless and gave the next orders before he pulled the entire fleet out of UK waters to enforce the quarantine.

Four torpedoes were fired in two rapid pairs, each targeted on the unsuspecting destroyer. The rippling, rolling explosions struck in sequence from bow to stern and transformed the warship into a mass of black smoke and fire.

In the ensuing chaos of the ship sinking, one dull grey helicopter, flying low over the water heading north, went unnoticed as the combined NATO fleet abandoned the UK mainland to push further out to sea and leave the entire UK and European continent to its fate.

As soon as they had withdrawn sufficient distances, another order was given and each person on board the ships in the fleet turned their eyes away as the evening horizon blossomed brightly with huge mushroom clouds as the nukes of the Soviets and the Americans detonated in a spectacular display of the destructiveness of humankind.

CHAPTER

NINE

"Sir? One Troop are reporting in," Daniels said to Captain Palmer, who switched channels and responded. Daniels listened in as he was still on that channel, but Johnson watched their faces for any sign of bad news. Hearing the end of the one-sided exchange, and understanding Palmer's orders for the two Fox cars to return to their position, he waited for the update.

"As bad as we suspected," Palmer said to Johnson, "the bridge is cut, heavy damage and a fire burning near the causeway, and there appears to be a rolling small arms battle going on."

"Helicopters?" Johnson asked.

"Nothing yet, and unable to raise them. I fear that our specialist colleagues may be right."

"About what, Sir?" Johnson asked.

"About having to have a *redundancy*. About setting up on our own and accepting our fate, if you will."

Johnson frowned deeply, only inside so that his face remained a resolute mask of professionalism and efficiency, as befitted his rank and position.

"With all due respect, Sir," he began, "those bloody ballerinas from Hereford can fu—"

"*Mister* Johnson," Palmer interjected sharply, "firstly, I believe our situation negates the need for such manners; if you wish to disagree with me simply state your opinion without adding your due respect. Secondly, I would suggest refraining from such opinions about the Special Air Service. They have just conducted a rather admirable action on our behalf, and also," he paused theatrically and looked up at the open hatch before adding in a lower voice, "you never know when they're listening."

"Very well, Sir," Johnson said as he tried to hide a small smile at the weak jest, "I believe that we should not give up on the island for a few reasons. Namely that the majority of our fighting strength is still there, not to mention the men's families and over a hundred civilians. Regardless of whether we can rescue any arms or armour, we shouldn't abandon this area until we know for certain. Sir."

"Noted, SSM," Palmer responded flatly, re-establishing the hierarchy with a simplistic grace.

"Thank you, Sir," Johnson responded, climbing out of the Sultan to check on his men, to perform some useful activity and prevent his mind from overflowing through his mouth. He didn't make it all of the way out before the radio sparked to life so loudly that he heard the tinny rattle from the headphones from half outside the hatch. Dropping back down, he saw Daniels had snatched up the set and had one earphone pressed to his left ear. His right hand scribbled furiously with pencil on a pad of paper as his mouth hung open. Palmer and Johnson watched on, neither of them breathing. A metallic shriek forced Daniels to drop the headset and pull his head away as he screwed up his eyes. Palmer and Johnson waited in the sudden silence of the interior of the tracked vehicle as their radio operator turned to face them.

"It's…" he began, before swallowing and composing himself, "It's the Russians. And the Americans. They've launched nuclear strikes."

"Where?" Palmer said, almost jumping out of his seat.

"On who?" Johnson said at the same time, bombarding the Corporal, who was forced to hold up both hands to ward off the questions for a moment as he closed his eyes and took a breath.

"They didn't know for sure," he said in a low voice cracking with stress, "but it isn't us. They think the Soviets launched on Europe to stop the advance and the Americans launched on them, thinking they were retaliating against Ivan launching."

More silence hung in the cramped, oily confines of the command vehicle until broken by the Captain.

"So, we are largely unaffected then?" he asked hopefully.

"I doubt it," Johnson muttered sourly, his face no longer hiding his opinion.

"The message said that they've cut us off. We're quarantined. Nothing in or out," Daniels finished ominously.

"Quarantined? Bloody *quarantined,*" Johnson snarled. He glanced to their officer, who simply sat with his head in his hands and said nothing. "Sir?"

Palmer looked up, suddenly appearing more exhausted than he had ever looked before, as though the combined weight of the last month of fighting, the implied loss of his only remaining family member and the three days without proper sleep, had all hit him at once.

"I had a fear this would happen," he said in a small voice. "It appears that the right hand is unaware of what the left hand is doing. Either that or the right hand no longer cares about the left."

Johnson guessed that they were the metaphorical left hand

in this ambiguous description, but the first thing that the captain had said worried him deeply.

"*What* would happen, Sir?" he asked carefully.

"It's what senior command called, rather melodramatically I thought at the time, I might add, their *Doomsday Protocol,*" he admitted in a voice almost inappropriately laced with humour. "When we were initially deployed to the city to exert control, there were fears of our lack of ability to contain the outbreak. I had assumed after the events of the last month that they had abandoned the idea, but it seems that I was wrong. Major Hadlington and I discussed the possibility, and he assured me that command at sea were no longer considering it."

"What is the Doomsday Protocol, Sir? Precisely?" Johnson asked, not truly wanting the answer but knowing that he had to ask.

"To sever all physical ties between the UK and the rest of the world. To literally cut off our island and let whatever it was burn itself out. It seemed that the cat was somewhat let out of the bag, given that Europe is gone, so I had assumed that the plan was shelved. It seems in that assumption that I was mistaken. Either that or the plan has been widened to incorporate the rest of Europe."

"Makes sense," Daniels mumbled to himself, prompting both senior men to turn and regard him.

"Elucidate, if you please, Corporal?" Palmer asked, making Daniels turn to Johnson for a translation.

"Explain," the SSM said simply, bridging the gap between Sandhurst and a basic secondary school education.

"Well, as far as we know, it hasn't spread to the yanks," Daniels said, "not unless they bring it back from here. If I was them, I'd blockade the whole bloody Atlantic and bomb the shit out of everywhere where the Screechers are... alive... or whatever it is."

The Captain and the Squadron Sergeant Major regarded

each other, agreeing with the simple sentiment with a casual tilt of the head.

"So what does that mean for us?" Johnson said out loud, half verbalising his own thought process and half asking.

"Not a great deal in the immediate," Palmer said, suddenly more confident and alert as though he had shaken off his brief funk of self-pity and concern. "We still have to find a way to get as many people off the island as we can and find a position to occupy until all this nonsense blows over."

The stereotypical upper-class frippery in his tone gave Johnson a bizarre sense of hope, of reassurance and even eagerness, which he knew was partly down to the faith he had in the officer who was never originally his.

"I'll see to the men," he said, excusing himself with an unnecessary task to fill his time, and climbing out of the vehicle.

Turning to the map on the wall and tracing the contour lines instinctively to find higher ground, Palmer selected three options within a close enough radius, utilising Daniels' local knowledge on a few points, then called for Downes and the freshly returned Sergeant Strauss to join them.

The cramped interior was made far worse, forcing Daniels to climb out to allow the others to see the map. The three locations were marked and briefed, designated as Alpha, Bravo and Charlie, as was the ingrained army way, and Strauss' troop were deployed with the SAS team to assess and secure any site that would suit their needs.

Just as they deployed, the hope of further bodies to bolster their number became a stronger reality as the radio burst into life once more.

———

Sergeant Horton, having survived the collapse of the bridge

and escaped the sinking tank, blackened by soot and smoke and streaked with white lines of sweat, turned his head from left to right. The Sterling machine gun, devoid of a magazine, hung from his right shoulder and clanged against his body awkwardly with every faltering step he took. With four other soldiers, he advanced up the hill away from the bright flames of the burning buildings near the short end of the bridge. Behind them, zombies poured from the beach unimpeded by anything but the barrier of broken bodies and the remnants of the fences, as they came on and tangled themselves in the ragged collection of ruined corpses and loosely-strung barbed-wire. They crawled over the other bodies of their kind to spill a mess of clawing, gnashing, screeching and hissing meat onto the cobbles.

Horton turned away, still followed by the three men in army uniform who took his lead unthinkingly. Ahead of them, far ahead and out of reach, a large huddle of men stood shoulder to shoulder, facing outwards as they made slow but defended progress up the street towards the higher ground. Others occasionally ran to them, bursting from buildings to run desperately and push through the ranks of their outward-facing formation and into the safety of the interior. Horton ignored the sprawling crowd filling the lowest part of the island and turned to break into a sluggish jog up the slope. The forgotten machine gun banged into him rhythmically as he moved faster than the three soldiers following him, to stretch out a lead. The rattling intensity of the gunfire ahead of the sergeant rose and fell as new threats emerged to be rapidly put down with disciplined fire.

Rising above the noise of the different calibre weapons was another sound. The loud, clear voice shouted out directions of zombies as they moved. The voice directed the entire ragged array of people as they bunched up and moved as one organism with its beating heart barking orders from within.

Horton moved as fast as he could, alone now as his three followers had dropped back so far as to not be in a position to offer him any support. Heading for the centre of the noise, for the beating heart of the group, a scream to his left made his head whip around to fix on the source of it. A door slammed, and Horton swerved without thinking to burst through it. Emerging into the light of the headquarters building, he fixed his eyes on the woman leaning over the desk, her hand clamped around the radio handset as she yelled words that he didn't understand. She turned and saw him, her eyes recognising Horton's cloudy orbs staring back at her over his torn face and blood-sheeted chest, and taking in the gore splashed down his uniform from the hole in his neck, she swore as he drew back bloody lips over red-stained teeth. She let out a shriek of pure horror before he flew at her.

———

"Convoy, this is the island," snapped the female radio operator with such panic or undisciplined radio protocols that the beginning and end of the transmission were cut off. The voice transmitting didn't wait for any acknowledgement, but simply ploughed on with the remainder of the hurried message. She had emerged from the toilet where she had been shoved, no doubt saving her life from the sounds of screams and ripping death in the room outside.

"We're overrun, and… oh, *fuck n...*"

The transmission died, as unbeknown to Daniels, Johnson and Palmer, the operator died only seconds afterwards, and at the hands, *teeth*, of a man they all knew. The three men exchanged looks, as if the bad situation they all knew about had suddenly become much worse, and all three of them knew how powerless they were to help.

"Ghostrider to any of you tank-monkeys still breathing

air," said the headset, before any of them could utter a word about the last transmission. Behind the cocky voice and disregard for operational radio use was the unmistakable whine, the high-pitched screaming of jet engines spooling up, and rotor blades spinning.

"Morris?" Palmer said into the radio, forgetting his own discipline and committing the cardinal sin of using names over the air. "Is that you? What's going on?"

"We're here," Morris replied in a suddenly serious voice, the sound of the engines rising further, "give me a grid and get ready to receive incoming."

Palmer shot a glance at the map on the wall before Johnson spoke up.

"Not here," he said, earning an annoyed look from the Captain. He kept his explanation brief and spoke succinctly.

"We don't have the transport or the safety here. We need somewhere to defend and resupply before we take on more people."

Palmer thought for a second, his young brow furrowed with the effort of rapid calculations, before turning back to Johnson.

"The camp?"

"It's our best bet, and it's close," the SSM replied, making Palmer glance back to the map wall to convey the grid coordinates for Daniels to relay.

Back to where we bloody started, Johnson thought depressingly, *and in shit state, too.*

CHAPTER

TEN

Kimberley, hatchet in hand and slipping in her sweaty grip, led her line of people through the narrow, cobbled pathways that ran between the back yards of the terraced houses. Twice she had nearly beheaded or bludgeoned innocent refugees, all running away from the noises of the raging battle below. The second person she raised the axe to, lowering it as soon as the string of expletives made it obvious that the shadow was alive, told her about the explosion and the fire at the bridge. In the wan light, her eyes locked once with Ashdown, who shook his head slowly to tell her that their slim plan for escape by vehicle was dead before it had truly begun.

A shriek in a street behind them made everyone flinch and duck down. Children began to cry, and heads turned back to the fierce woman they seemed to have collectively decided was in charge. Kimberley looked to Ashdown, who was being tended to by his wife as he rested against a wall and breathed heavily, evidently still not recovered from his injuries and near-fatal encounter.

Taking the initiative, she snapped her fingers twice to make the small noise echo loudly along the stone corridor over the raging sounds of the battle below.

"Follow me," she hissed loudly, "we're going uphill towards the helicopter."

Her column grew with each occupied house they passed, until she led over twenty people upwards into the night. She had no idea why she chose to put their collective faith and safety in a guess, a desperate hope that they could evacuate by air. The alternative was certain death, but the confidence they all showed in her decision was almost palpable. Inside, her mind screamed in fear and self-doubt, but outwardly she led.

And they followed.

———

"This way!" Lieutenant Palmer hissed at the line of civilians skulking through the darkened alleyways. He had gathered a collection, mostly the old and the young and the infirm, but he had managed to threaten and cajole the men of Three Troop to move whatever vehicles they could, and to abandon those that they could not. All around him, men cowered behind low walls and behind coal bunkers with their weapons pointed nervously downhill.

"I say," he said more insistently, his nasal voice cutting the air at the perfect tone to whip Kimberley's head around to look at him. Lieutenant Palmer flinched in fright at the speed that the face turned and seemed to look directly at him. Logic cut in on the dance between sense and fear skipping fast through his mind, and it reminded him that the Screechers didn't carry weapons and walk low to the ground to hide their presence.

He waved them over, seeing the few become over twenty.

"Lieutenant?" Kimberley asked, recognising the shape of the man and his voice even though the gathering dark prevented her from making out his features in any great detail.

"Indeed," Palmer replied, "get your people under cover and keep them quiet. We will have to move shortly."

"*My* peop…" Kimberley started to say before she was cut off.

"We are heading for the landing area. We at least have one helicopter left and I'm hoping that we can get as many of us off this cursed rock as possible."

With that, he turned away from her and left her to repeat the whispered message to every third person that slunk past her.

"Stay hidden. Keep quiet; we're getting out of here."

Lieutenant Palmer, pulse racing and the weight of command pressing down heavily on his shoulders, took three soldiers at random to accompany him and for the first time in his brief military career, he wished that he had taken the time to get to know the names of the men under him. At least he did, now that he had to rely on them to save his life if the need arose.

He moved low, ignoring the trained cautions that the more experienced soldiers had ingrained when it came to exposed areas and corners. Palmer's lack of military experience made his progress faster, and ultimately safer as this new enemy did not set up ambushes or use ranged weapons. The key here was speed and stealth, weighing up one against the other to remain undetected. He was certain that none of them had infiltrated this high up the hill, but the sounds of gunfire from below grew steadily louder as that fight headed unavoidably upwards. The hulking silhouette of the ungainly and bulbous helicopter tickled the skyline ahead of him, lit by occasional flashes from behind him, and set against the lighter sky over the sea. The sound of a weapon cocking rang out at the same time as a challenge pierced the air a little louder than was necessary.

"Put that down, man!" Palmer snapped at Brinklow, the loadmaster now famous thanks to his musical escapades at the first battle for the island, and who had already been serving in the Royal Navy when the officer was born.

"Sorry, Sir, Mister Barrett and Mister Morris are ready to start pre-flight," he said, turning to point uselessly into the dark. As soon as he had said this, the pilot appeared and called out to see who it was.

"Lieutenant Palmer, Sir," Palmer said respectfully, almost pronouncing the slight bow of aristocracy in his DNA, "We have almost forty people not far away; soldiers and civilians."

Lieutenant Commander Barrett was silent for a moment before responding.

"Depending on how far we evacuate, we can take thirty at a time, just so long as they aren't carrying too much equipment," he said after the brief mental calculations.

"Where to, Sir?" Palmer asked.

Barrett didn't respond, merely climbed back aboard the aircraft. A pregnant pause of no more than twenty seconds elapsed, then a loud noise made them all flinch in the dark as the helicopter's engines sparked into sudden, raucous life. Barret dropped back down and ran over to put his mouth to Palmer's ear.

"Get everyone up here," he said, "we're going to rendezvous with the remainder of the armour that went to London."

Palmer nodded and turned away, his mind registering but ignoring the comment about his brother's column only having a *remainder* of its original strength.

Barrett climbed back into the fuselage and settled himself into the figure-hugging seat high up in the cockpit. He lifted on his headset and listened in to the end of the conversation his co-pilot was having with the older brother of the army officer he had just sent away.

"Roger," Morris said over the radio, "Ghostrider, out."

"I do wish you wouldn't call us that, Morris," Barrett said

in mild annoyance as he strapped in and flicked switches. "Where are they?"

"Not sure, precisely," Morris responded as he worked his own controls, "but they have given us an RV point to start dropping people and they're on their way as we speak."

"Did they say why?" Barrett asked.

"Indefensible position, I should imagine, but they didn't specify," Morris responded and kicked the engine speed up a little further.

"Gary?" Barrett said into the microphone attached into his helmet, speaking over the operational open-mic for their crew.

"Go on," Brinklow said.

"Prepare to load thirty at a time and make sure you make the first batch heavy with soldiers to secure the RV."

"Understood," Brinklow answered.

"Flight time?" Barrett asked Morris.

"A little under five minutes. I'd estimate a fifteen-minute turnaround, tops."

"Okay, first load expected any time soon. Let's get them the hell out of here."

"Okay everyone," Palmer announced peevishly, "follow me, if you please. We will get you all evacuated in batches, so I ask that you not push one another, and follow instructions."

He turned to lead them away, hearing the muttered insults aimed at his back and chose to pretend that he didn't hear them. One man, however, stood tall and spoke at a normal volume, which earned hisses of shushing from everyone in earshot.

"Me and my wife have to be on the first flight," he began, prompting even the seemingly-arrogant Lieutenant Palmer to stare at him in shock, "my wife is pregnant," he insisted, with a face that not even he could keep straight.

Palmer glanced at the woman, clearly more than double the officer's age and with a noticeably flat stomach, as she tried to pull her husband's arm away, looking at the man with an incredulous stare of mixed disgust and horror.

"Madam," Palmer said, echoing some of the exquisite manners and gallantry of his older brother, "my congratulations to you and your husband, but please be patient with our efforts to evacuate everyone." With that, he turned away and called for a sergeant to relay his instructions. Those instructions were accepted and followed, leaving him almost shocked that assuming control of the men was so easy. His mood dropped instantly, knowing that the two intimidating sergeants in his squadron weren't present, not to mention the SSM or Palmer's own brother, who he knew the men would follow without question and with something bordering on adoration. The knowledge that he was the best choice for leadership in a pool of one left him a little soured, but he knew he had no time for self-pity.

The group made their slow progress uphill, unimpeded by the undead that tore the lower slopes apart in their unending quest for living flesh. The first thirty bodies were loaded onto the helicopter and the door slid noisily shut before the engines screamed intensely as the wheels squeaked on their suspension shocks in take-off. The noise was incredible, making everyone duck their heads low as the sound of the helicopter faded away to leave them in the relatively quiet darkness. The gunfire still sounded loudly from below them as they began their agonising wait for the aircraft to return.

———

"I'm out!" shouted a marine desperately from Lieutenant Lloyd's right side.

"Here, lad," came his sergeant's implacable voice, "don't bloody waste 'em."

Lloyd smiled despite the situation, ever grateful for the

squat and seemingly indestructible NCO who kept his men in top condition at all times. He knew that the fatherly sergeant would have a number of spare items on or about his person that the lads would either have a habit of losing or forgetting. He had probably stuffed a half-dozen spare magazines for their rifles down the top of his camouflaged smock, on top of the full pouches he had. At any one time the man probably had the equipment of two marines in his possession.

"Civvies on the left!" came another shout, making their officer turn to face that direction. The twenty men he had under his unorthodox command were roughly half and half marines and army, and of the latter he could only tell who was who due to their different weapon reports. The front door of a nearby building was open, showing two frightened faces in the light of their sporadic muzzle flashes.

"Split!" Lloyd called out, pushing his way into the outer rank to force a gap and began waving the survivors out of their hiding place and towards the dubious safety of his flock of armed sheep. They ran, no hesitation or delay, and piled into the formation only for it to close up like some previously unknown single-celled organism. They had almost the same number of civilians huddled together in the middle, and the majority of the fighting was directed back downhill where a loose gaggle of zombies advanced well ahead of the tidal wave still pouring from the now open beachhead.

"Mark your shots, boys," Lloyd called out to reassure them, only to be heard so that they knew they were still led by someone confident. Their slow retreat moved at the same speed as the mass of the main advance, and soon their only contact was with the surprise arrivals of people who used to be their own and the few faster ones. Lloyd was reminded of that additional danger by a shout from their front rank facing the main assault.

"Lima breaking out!" came the shout, "and it's bringing more with it!"

Lloyd was preparing to call a halt and drop his front rank to their knees to meet the renewed foray, but another voice called over the din.

"Keep going, I'll get the fucker," said Enfield, his cool-headed sniper, who pushed ahead and sat back on his right foot with his left knee up to steady the long barrel of the big rifle he unslung from his shoulder. His spotter and constant shadow advanced a few paces with him, also dropping down to kneel and scan his weapon over his sniper's head to deal with any threats that presented themselves to them.

Over the tumult of noises, a single, booming report echoed over the rest, followed by a crisp shout of, "Lima down," as the two men jogged back to the safety of the huddle. Looking ahead to the area lit by the raging fire, Lloyd saw that the vanguard that had flowed out of the main group, hot on the tails of their leader, now faltered and milled about. Around him, the firing had ceased and was replaced only with the crying of the refugees and the clicks and scrapes of weapons reloading.

"Keep moving!" he called, just as they noticed the growing sounds of a rotary wing aircraft surging back over their heads to flare in high above them to land on the island.

CHAPTER

ELEVEN

The first load to disgorge from the belly of the aircraft spilled out into the darkness, led by Sergeant Rod Sinclair and half a dozen of his troop, to spread out and adopt defensive positions as the unarmed civilians huddled together. Satisfied that the area was clear after the silence resumed from the harsh invasion of the helicopter, he sent three of his men to open and clear a large, low hangar building, as others activated a few flares so that the returning helicopter could find them easily.

Alone with only what they carried on their backs and feeling abandoned in the dark, they prayed for the aircraft to return soon.

———

"I hear them," a trooper said beside Lieutenant Palmer, who craned his neck up to concentrate on the sounds in the air until he could hear the thudding whine of the rotors at the edge of his hearing. He turned to the group, guessing he had maybe two more loads until they were safely away from the infected and cut-off island. He had heard the battle below them appearing to grind to a halt, and the cessation of regular gunfire, and had assumed that whatever resistance still lived down there was overrun by now. As the helicopter flared and touched down, he counted off another thirty as he slapped their backs and shouted the number out loud. He got to twenty-five and held up an arm to stop the civilians advancing, nodding to a group of soldiers standing ready to climb aboard. The man he had stopped pushed him off balance, shouting. Palmer righted himself and pushed back, finding himself outweighed and shorter than the man. The helicopter took off, leaving him with only a handful of soldiers at his disposal as the man surged forward to push him again.

"We should have been on that helicopter!" raged the man, "my wife is *pregnant!*"

"No, I'm not, Gordon," snapped the woman beside him as she tried to pull his arm back. He shook her off angrily, raising the back of one hand towards her in the dull glow of a light bathing the landing area in a weak yellow. His wife shrank back instantly and cowered, displaying the measure of a man her husband was in front of everyone watching. Palmer drew himself up and spoke loudly.

"Now, look here, Sir," he said haughtily, unable to get another word out as the man punched him squarely on the nose and felled him like a small tree. Screams erupted from the group in response, and the injured Graham Ashdown limped forwards to stand between the young officer and his attacker.

"I know you're scared, mate," he said with his hands held out, "we all are, but there's no need for that."

"You can fuck off, too," snarled the man as he stepped forwards and snatched for Ashdown's gun and knocked him down on top of Palmer, making both men cry out.

Another noise cut over those sounds and brought with it a

stunned silence. The sound was a strangled cry, punctuated with a gasping choke and an unmistakable whimper of terror. Palmer and Ashdown righted themselves and looked up to see the man on his knees with eyes as wide and bright as headlamps on a truck. The only thing brighter than those eyes was the slither of sharpened metal at the edge of an axe blade which was hooked around his windpipe and forcing him to remain very, *very* still. Kimberley tossed her hair out of her face, for the first time revealing the entirety of the scar running into her hairline and distorting the shape of her ear. She leaned down and whispered in the man's ear, making his eyes widen that little bit further. Without another audible word, the young woman straightened and released him by removing the weapon. The main put both hands to his throat and got unsteadily to his feet to stagger away to the back of the group, as Kimberley took his wife gently by the arm and deposited her with Denise and the others of her original group. Returning to Ashdown, she helped the injured man to his feet and then looked down to extend a hand to the young officer. Taking it, he was shocked to feel the strength in her grip as she hauled him up, looking him directly in the eye as she spoke.

"There is only one way to deal with a bully, Lieutenant," she said with edged steel in her voice, "and that is to scare them more than they scare others."

With that unexpected advice given, she turned away and walked tall back to her small huddle that was comforting the woman she had just publicly removed from her abuser, to wait in silence for the last ride out of that hell-hole.

———

"On the right!" called out an RMP, his scarlet beret still sitting atop his head perfectly above a stained face that looked calmly over the long barrel of his heavy rifle. Lloyd followed the sound of the voice and looked beyond, seeing a small crowd of bloodied uniforms mobbing something or someone.

"Hold!" he bellowed, feeling the formation halt awkwardly.

"You, you and you," he said, slapping the backs of the nearest soldiers, of whom only one was originally his own, "with me. Spikes only unless you absolutely have to," he finished, telling them to use their bayonets and not to fire and attract attention unless it was vital.

They advanced, still unnoticed by the small mob of former colleagues and civilians who pushed at a door hungrily. The door was not barred or closed, and each surging attempt to gain entry was rewarded with a flash of light from within. Lloyd looked at his three soldiers, his own eyes trying to radiate calm when theirs were wide in terror, and he pointed to the bayonets on the end of their guns, then to the base of his neck and to the backs of the zombies who were still unaware of their presence. They nodded and the four of them advanced in a cautious line, just as the door was ripped inwards and two bayonets were thrust forward to spear the faces of the leading zombies. The two crowding behind them eager for fresh meat fell inwards to sprawl on the floor, and they fell to the blades as they punctured the skulls of the downed enemies. To Lloyd's total surprise, a tall man with a shock of white hair emerged from the doorway wielding the most unexpected weapon he had seen used in his life.

Colonel Tim lay waste to three zombies standing before him with the heavy Scottish claymore blade, severing two heads with clean swings and driving the wide point straight through an eye socket to burst the blade out of the rear of his attacker's head, with a shout of pure rage to kill the last of the group.

Seeing the four men with raised weapons ahead of him, the rictus of war left his face almost immediately as his genial smile returned.

"Bagged two brace of the blighters now," he said gleefully, as though proud of his achievements on an organised hunt, rather than fighting for the survival of the human race against the undead. "Still, I imagine you chaps have plenty under your belts by the look of you?"

"Er, yes, Sir," Lloyd said, "would you come with us, Colonel?"

"Of course. Good idea, er, Lieutenant?"

"Lloyd, Sir," he replied, disbelieving even his own polite words in the midst of what they were going through, "if you wouldn't mind?" he said, gesturing for the senior officer to accompany him back to the loose rally square on the main street.

"Come on, you two," the Colonel announced over his shoulder to the two privates assigned to keep him out of trouble. They stooped to pick up bags, no doubt the Colonel's chess set or fine china instead of anything useful, and they re-joined the group.

"Fine show, boys!" the Colonel announced as he smiled at the terrified faces, "top shelf!"

Chuckles rippled through the loose ranks in spite of the gravity of the situation, and Lloyd swore he could have heard one of the reservists mutter, "Typical bloody Rupert. There should be one of them puppets of him on that Spitting Image on the telly."

"Up we go, everyone," Lloyd said, seeing how alarmingly fast the main group of zombies had advanced as they had been stationary.

———

"Up we go," Lieutenant Palmer announced in ignorant echo of his royal marine counterpart on the slope below him, as he counted another thirty onto the helicopter, leaving only himself and two others on the cobbles. Looking up at the loadmaster and seeing the mental calculations going on, he read the answer in the man's eyes and turned back to get the last two on board. As he turned, he saw a sight that filled his heart with happiness, and then sank it to the soles of his boots because he knew that he was in for a fight.

"Every man with a weapon to get off *right now*," he screamed up at Brinklow, who nodded and went inside to physically remove the soldiers from the aircraft and propel them towards the door. Palmer pushed them away from the aircraft where he arranged them into a loose line.

"Don't bloody look at me, face front, damn you!" he bawled, finding a gravelly edge to his usually genteel voice. The confused soldiers, all of them having thought themselves safe from the horrors they were about to escape, now found that they were thrust back into the fight under the leadership of a man who was as untested as he was disliked.

As their new and unwelcome reality dawned on them, their eyes spied the formation heading for them in the gloom of the slope leading to the base of the island.

Palmer, having seen and recognised what was heading for them, had made the decision to stay behind and fight a last stand in the hopes of saving more people, but as soon as he shouted his last instructions to the helicopter's loadmaster and shielded his face as the huge aircraft surged upwards, he felt suddenly and terribly alone; as though he had just condemned all of them. Looking around and wishing he had kept one of the sergeants to lead the men with him.

Or for *me, more like,* he thought sourly he watched in horror as the men somehow organised themselves.

"Take aim," one of them shouted, as Palmer saw them raise their weapons to their shoulders. He opened his mouth, desperately willing himself to find his voice before the order to fire was given, when another voice cut the air like the tearing of sheet metal.

"No!" the voice shrieked, higher pitched and lacking the baritone edge usually expected with battlefield orders. "They're still alive!"

Palmer turned to see Kimberley beside him, shoulders back and head high, with a small axe gripped firmly in her right hand. Before Palmer could utter a word in support, the men realised their mistake. Guns were lowered, and hushed shouts of encouragement rang out to bring the large knot of men to them.

"Identify yourselves," one nervous soldier shouted.

"Fuck that, mate," came the breathless and unexpectedly thick Midlands accent of a man emerging from the darkness dressed as a royal marine, "give us a gap, like?"

The men split in the centre, allowing the formation to pour through like a large-scale display of water moving between cells in the body. The front line closed up again, swelled and extended by the addition of over a dozen fighting men.

"Who's in charge here?" called a confident voice, if a little ragged and out of breath.

"I am," Palmer said, feeling suddenly threatened by a real soldier challenging his authority, "and have we not set a formal challenge and password?" he said, surprising even himself with how obnoxious he sounded.

"That you, Palmer?" Lieutenant Lloyd asked as he rested his hands on his knees briefly. Palmer said nothing, merely cleared his throat with a sound that reminded him of a small dog attempting to be threatening.

"If you haven't noticed, man, we're not fighting the bloody Russians," Lloyd said with gentle mockery that lacked the tone of confrontation, "and I doubt these bastards are trying to infiltrate our lines. Do you?"

Palmer was left dumbstruck by his own stupidity and had to admit that it was unlikely.

"Quite," was all that he said by way of admission, "what happened at the bridge?"

"Bloody artillery shell dropped the causeway," Lloyd said, "and somehow they got behind our defences. So many went into the water that they piled up on the beach and poured through the fences. We could've held them, but they started coming from behind us."

"Is this everyone?" another voice asked, cutting over them both. Lloyd stood up straight on hearing the voice, in spite of not being able to fully see the speaker.

"Everyone we could save, yes," he answered solemnly.

"We had close to four hundred people here," Kimberley said, "and now we've sent out sixty with what? One more load to go out?"

"I apologise," Lloyd said with the slightest hint of warning in his voice, "we did what we could."

"I'm not criticising," she said, "I'm sorry if it sounded that way, it's just that the helicopter can take thirty people if they aren't carrying much with them. We have forty five people here as far as I can count, and most of them have weapons," she said, leaving the implication open and obvious.

Palmer and Lloyd locked eyes in the low light available from the dull light source near the makeshift landing pad.

"What's the turnaround time?" Lloyd asked.

"Fifteen, give or take," Palmer answered as both men lapsed into silence as they figured it would be over ten minutes before the helicopter returned, close to fifteen before it departed and a full thirty before the final sortie flew and evacuated the last of the living from the island. That realisation hit both men at once and both turned to shout orders to the men holding the ragged line.

"Grab anything you can for a barricade!" Lloyd called out.

"Dig in, chaps, anyone with grenades please shout up," Palmer said.

"I'll keep the others out of the way," said a female voice from behind them, then footsteps rattled away over the cobbles as Kimberley went about her own self-appointed duties.

"This is going to be tight," Lloyd said.

"Indeed," Palmer concurred.

CHAPTER

TWELVE

"Roger, ETA sixteen minutes. Out." Murray said into the radio, grimacing as he shifted his grip on the controls, making the airframe wobble slightly.

"Are you sure you are alright to fly?" Astrid Larsen asked, her shouted voice coming through the headset clearly.

"Madam!" Murray barked, his voice strained because of the pain and numbness coursing through his body, "I quite understand your concern, but the situation hardly allows that I can merely *pull over* and let someone else drive, does it?"

"You make a good point," Astrid said, ducking her head back out of the cockpit to return to the three men in the rear. She had been volunteered to check on their injured pilot after the turbulence had caused the two SBS men to actually sit down and strap in; a rarity with any special forces troops, in stark comparison to the regimented practices of their original units.

"He says that he is fine," she said to Berg in their native language in response to his raised eyebrow in the red-lit interior of the aircraft, then turned to the other occupants and explained in English.

"He says that he is okay," she said in English, raising her hand with her thumb and forefinger held together in a circle in the international scuba diving signal for 'okay'. She didn't quite believe his assurance, but as the pilot himself pointed out, there was no other choice as there wasn't much in the way of rest areas in the English Channel. They needed to get to dry land and they had precisely one choice in pilots, which is why all four surviving special forces commandos strapped in and hoped for the best.

———

"Who is in charge here?" Captain Palmer called out in echoing similarity to the struggle unfolding on the island, as he dismounted at the landing area back in the camp, where all of his surviving men had started their war, even if he hadn't.

"Sir," a voice called from the darkness.

"On me, man," Palmer snapped. Sergeant Sinclair jogged in, giving the report of the action on the island, the abandoned equipment, the airlifts, and most worryingly about the outbreak.

"Second load just arrived, Sir," he said, "expecting the last in roughly fifteen."

"Understood, Sergeant, thank you. SSM?"

"Sir?" Johnson said from directly behind the man, not waiting respectfully out of earshot, as he wasn't a fan of second-hand information.

"Mister Johnson, I'll trouble you to take on the defences here, if you don't mind?"

"Very good, Sir," Johnson said as he turned away, "Maxwell? All round defence. Protect this LZ until the rest are evacced from the island. We can't see for shit, so it looks like we're holding this position until daybreak, which is," he paused to look at the luminescent tips on the hands of his watch, "eight hours at least."

"Will do," Maxwell said, the unspoken stress of his own family's welfare only just creeping into his voice, but not affecting his abilities as a soldier. Johnson listened as Maxwell went along the perimeter to arrange the men in pairs, unable to see his work well, so relying on his other senses.

"Sarn't Major?" said a voice from his left, making him turn.

"Who's that?" he growled, perhaps a little more harshly than he expected the words would come out.

"Sinclair," came the response.

"Rod. How are your boys holding up?" Johnson asked, meaning the question to be aimed directly at the NCO, but allowing him to give his answer on behalf of Two Troop. It was the original, 'asking for a friend' hypothetical question.

"They were pretty rattled, to be honest. Better now, now that we're away and out of the fight for now," he answered, giving the answer that Johnson expected; that Rod Sinclair was terrified but holding it together, just as his boys were.

"We've got a building open, Sarn't Major," he went on, "and there's a brew on if you wanted one?"

"Good man. Civvies ok?"

"Not the best," Sinclair answered, his voice giving the indication in the dark that his brow was well and truly knitted, "lots of us and them left behind, if you know what I mean."

"What's the bill so far?" Johnson asked, meaning the butcher's bill of losses.

"There's another load on their way hopefully, but we'll be lucky if we've come out with a quarter…"

Johnson said nothing, only stayed stock still and absorbed the fact that they had seventy-five percent less life to protect. Those figures swam in his head and tortured him as he tried to imagine the secondary losses; that of the number of fighting men lost and no longer a resource to protect the others. That train of thought delved deeper into his sudden depression as he considered how many of his men would be fighting-fit after the inevitable loss of their loved ones. He thought of the blame, of the bitterness as men struggled to cope with grief and anger.

"Sarn't Major?" Sinclair said, interrupting his thoughts and bringing him back to the moment.

"Sorry, yes, thank you," he answered hurriedly, "I'll have Maxwell take over out here if you wouldn't mind arranging things inside? Keep them quiet and calm?"

"Will do."

Johnson listened as Sinclair walked away, pushing down his own feelings as far as he could to survive the night and start afresh in the daylight. He wanted to let someone else decide, wanted to crawl under a rock or just use one to bash his own head in for the failures and the losses. He paced, cursing himself for anything he could have or should have done differently. He should have pushed to have them all evacuated weeks ago, should've refused to accept the orders to sit tight and wait for all this nonsense to blow over so that the BBC could resume their normal, polite service and tell people not to panic. As he paced, a smell hit his nostrils and reminded him of the rank insignia on his uniform, kicking back into the role of the Squadron Sergeant Major; a man with the senses of superman, able to detect the lowest of mutterings over distance, and now, in this case, the unmistakable smell of burning tobacco.

He stalked the defensive positions like a hunting bear; soft-footed and slightly crouched, moving carefully so that his equipment didn't rattle and betray his approach. His nose led him directly to a position occupied by two men, but their low conversation didn't identify them to his ears. The faint cherry-red glow of the tip of a lit cigarette was what had sparked his senses, and the anger he felt for the breach of routine was heightened to a fury, given the situation. Careful not to be in a position where he could be shot or run-through with a bayonet when he startled the men, he crept close and put his face between their heads, which faced outwards.

"You fucking idiot," he growled, feeling both men flinch and jump in terror, "if I can smell your bloody smokes, then what do you think the Screechers will do? Stroll up and offer you a light and then be on their merry way? For fuck's sake, I can smell you further away than a Union Street hooker's clout!"

The soldier, who had been attempting to hide his moment of stress-relieving indulgence by blowing the smoke inside his uniform coat, coughed and stubbed out the cigarette desperately as he tried not to breathe out. The smoke left in his lungs burned him as it leaked in small tendrils out of his nostrils.

"Hand them over," Johnson growled, hearing the rustling of clothing as the packet was placed carefully in his outstretched hand, "and the matches. I'm forced to trust you with a gun, but obviously trusting you with the ability to make fire is too much responsibility for one fucking moron."

A lighter was placed in his hand on top of the cigarettes.

"What about you?" Johnson said to the other soldier.

"Don't smoke, Sir," he whispered.

"No? But you didn't think to tell this waste of space not to?" he asked menacingly.

No answer came, so Johnson rose to his feet and slapped each man across the head before stalking away.

———

Both soldiers stayed frozen in position, unblinking and barely breathing.

"Where the fuck did he come from?" the now former smoker asked in a quiet voice.

"I have no idea," replied his mate, "but I'd rather go back

to the bloody island than get in the shit with him again, dickhead."

———

Johnson walked carefully back towards the darker shapes of the low buildings illuminated by the dull glow of the red light from the flares marking the landing zone. He walked inside, seeing a few shrouded lights with people huddled around them.

"Sergeant Croft?" he called out, getting no reply.

"Quartermaster?" he tried, hoping that Rochefort would at least be there.

Still no response.

"Corporal Mander?" he barked, a little louder now, hoping to find any of the men he had left in the island headquarters.

"Didn't make it, Sir," a trooper said from his position sitting by his right foot.

"You injured, trooper?" he asked in a neutral voice, ready to launch into a display should the man prove to be fighting-fit and avoiding the outside work.

"Ankle, Sir," he replied, gesturing at a foot strapped heavily with bandages raised on a wooden crate.

"Did you see it?" he asked quietly.

"No, Sir, but I saw a load of the bastards go into the HQ. Too many to…" he trailed away, suddenly feeling the pang of guilt and responsibility.

"It happened, son," Johnson said almost coldly, "no point in worrying about it now."

Unable to face the others and field more questions, he took himself away to a quiet corner of the large room and closed his hand around the cigarettes in his pocket. Suddenly stopping squeezing as he realised he was ruining a finite resource, he released them and gently extracted one from the packet and straightened it before putting the filter in his mouth and lighting it. He smoked half of it, suddenly no longer enjoying the harsh burn in his throat and chest and tossed it onto the concrete floor to grind it out with his boot, as though the action could assuage the myriad emotions he was experiencing.

Walking back outside, he passed the injured soldier again and tossed him the rest of the smokes without waiting to hear any thanks. As he walked towards the exit, a noise to his left in the darkness caught his finely-tuned ear and diverted him to investigate.

Pulling open boxes one at a time to try and find anything useful or at least valuable enough to trade, the man kept glancing behind his right shoulder as though he expected to be caught at

any point like a child raiding a biscuit tin. His glances towards the obvious route showed his inexperience, as the sound of a throat clearing behind his other shoulder made him spin and bring up the bayonet he was using to pry open crates.

Johnson caught the wrist holding the blade with ease, his large hand and fingers crushing the tendons to weaken the grip instantly to force the weapon to clatter to the ground, just as his right hand raised to grab the throat of the man. Two long strides forced him out of the shadows and into the weak light, and the recognition did not lower Johnson's blood pressure one bit.

"Trooper Nevin," he snarled, "kindly explain to me what you just did wrong?"

Nevin, as Johnson well knew, could not explain anything as the hand gripping his throat stopped all normal traffic of air and words. Whether he realised it or not, the question was not intended to be rhetorical.

"Nothing? I shall explain *for* you, then," Johnson said more loudly as he continued to march him backwards and choke the life out of him. "Firstly, you cowardly piece of shit, people need protecting and, much as I am ashamed to admit it, last time I checked, you were supposed to be a soldier and not a burglar. Secondly, you flap of gristle, you ever raise a hand to me again and I'll rip the fucking thing off and shove it up your arse. Sergeant Strauss?" he said, shouting the last two words louder than was sensible, but the rage was pouring out of him like steam by then. Boots sounded on concrete and three men appeared, Strauss at the head of them.

"Ah," Johnson said conversationally as Nevin's feet began to dance and his face turned purple, "I believe this is yours, Sergeant?"

"It is, Sir," Strauss said, his eyes promising punishment close to murder, "what was it doing?"

"I believe it was raiding the supplies here instead of doing its job. See to it that it finds itself in a particularly uncomfortable and dangerous position to prove to me that it is worth keeping around?"

"Yes, Sir," Strauss said, stepping forward to catch the collar of Nevin's jacket as the hand choking him opened. The loud gasp of involuntary air intake was cut short as he was hauled away backwards and dragged to the exterior perimeter to stand the rest of the night as sentry.

Johnson, still shaking with anger and emotion, had no time to dwell on the incident as he heard the far-off rhythmic thud of rotor blades.

Barrett, ignoring the professional pride of the flawless touchdown he normally observed, flared and dropped to the tarmac hard and powered down only just enough to keep the aircraft on the deck for as long as it took to unload their human cargo. Johnson jogged over, grabbing the loadmaster and shouting in his ear.

"I thought this was the last load?"

"No," Brinklow shouted back as he shook his head emphatically, "two more. The other aircraft is on the way back there now."

Johnson took this in as he watched the faces getting off the helicopter, seeing that not one of them was military, which meant that either all the rest of his men were lost or, more likely, that they were still there fighting, but now with dwindling numbers. He turned to shout another name.

"Captain Pa—"

"Here," Palmer shouted from directly beside him, craning up to lean his ear towards the bigger man and hear what he needed to say.

"Still one more load on the island. I'm going back with them," he shouted, stabbing a thumb over his shoulder at the helicopter.

Palmer absorbed this for a few seconds, then nodded once and held up a single finger before turning away and taking off at a jog. Johnson turned to the nearest trooper, pulling two spare magazines from the man's pouches before he hauled himself on board the aircraft, pausing as the loadmaster looked at him briefly and shrugged. Johnson turned back to see Palmer and two troopers with their arms full. Palmer passed up a dismounted GPMG, and then Johnson took the two full boxes of linked ammunition for the big gun. The last box had the lid lifted back for his inspection, and he kept his eyebrows raised as he looked back to the captain, who shot him a wink before retreating.

The engines screamed, and the ground fell away beneath Johnson's feet.

CHAPTER

THIRTEEN

"Here they come," Sergeant Hampton called out in warning, before leaning into his rifle and firing single shots at the heads illuminated by the fire hastily lit in a wheelbarrow further down the slope. The fire was a double-edged sword as the flickering flames no doubt attracted the zombies, but the payoff that the soldiers could see their targets was worth the disadvantage.

All along the weak barricade, men started to fire with him, striving to bring down the fastest moving zombies who had stretched far ahead of the mass rolling relentlessly uphill towards their last stand.

The only person not cowering in cover or firing over the barricade stood there feeling suddenly useless as she gripped the small axe in her sweaty palm. She looked around, left and right, desperately searching for anything that could be used to stem the tide of dead and help the fight. Shouts from the front sounded intermittently as men were pulled back from the centre of the line, having run out of ammunition. Each man withdrawn to stand as a second line, with bayonets ready, made Kimberley more and more fearful that they would be overrun before the helicopter returned, and she knew that she would be forced to retreat with the other civilians and abandon brave men to a fate she couldn't bring herself to imagine.

Before her nerve broke, the firing died off and she stepped cautiously forward to see that the advance line of zombies had been brought down.

"Ammo count!" Lloyd shouted.

Men fumbled in pouches, some bringing out a spare magazine and calling forward another soldier with the same kind of gun to thicken and strengthen the line, which still looked impossibly weak. She caught Lloyd's eye and saw the resignation, the acceptance there. She also saw from the glint in his eyes that he would not stop fighting.

"Eyes front!" Hampton shouted again, having finished dishing out the remainder of his ammunition to three marines who had joined him in the very centre of the barricade.

All eyes turned to the front, and all hearts sank as the advancing mass was lit up by a few light sources.

"Well, fuck my old boots," said one man on the front line.

"Now, now," Lieutenant Palmer admonished haughtily in an attempt at joining in the men's humour, "ladies present, boys. No need for barrack-room language."

"Sorry, Sir," quipped the man, "but there's a few of them."

A few of them was something of an understatement. Palmer and Lloyd both stared ahead before facing each other and guessing at numbers.

"Five hundred?" Palmer asked quietly.

"More," Lloyd said, before realising that Kimberley Perkins was standing within earshot.

"And how many bullets left?" she asked.

"Not nearly enough," Lloyd said with the same sad resignation his eyes had conveyed.

Kimberley bit her lip, making the two officers misunderstand and try to reassure her.

"Wait here," she said, then disappeared into the darkness further up the hill.

"Well, there isn't really anywhere else to be, is there, Christopher?" Palmer said with all the poise he could muster.

"No, Olly," he answered, "there bloody well isn't. Look alive, boys!" he called out, "All we have to do is hit three of them with each bullet!"

The weak ripple of laughter died away in Kimberley's ears as she ran up the slope, her eyes wide to try and make out the shapes of what she hoped to find. Single, loud shots sounded at regular intervals behind her, making her jump as she felt her way along in the darkness, eventually finding the slatted metal indicating what she wanted.

"Sir?" Marine Leigh called out as he lowered the small binoculars from his face, "He did it, Sir."

"Did what?" Lieutenant Lloyd asked as he stepped close.

"Did for three of the fuckers with one bullet," Leigh answered with a toothy grin as he nudged his head at their sniper, who rested the long barrel of his weapon over the barricade. It took a moment for Lloyd to understand that his jest had just been taken seriously, even more time to realise that it had been achieved, but he knew that if any of them could time an accurate shot to line up three of the shambling corpses for such a trick shot, then it was their implacably calm marine Enfield with his Accuracy International.

"Double rum ration for that man!" Palmer announced gleefully, earning an almost audible groan of embarrassment from the collection of men, mostly marines, at his attempt at a joke that was only a century out of date. As their groan died down, a louder, and infinitely more menacing groan rolled upwards to their tenuous position near the top of the hill.

Two other noises pricked the air at the same time; the unmistakable and heavenly sound of thudding helicopter blades and the unexpected sound of a big diesel engine barking into life.

As one, the men holding the thin line turned to the loudest and nearest source of sound, and saw headlights descending the hill towards them. They shielded their eyes from the bright lights as their night vision was instantly ruined, and the vehicle came to a squeaking halt before their meagre barricade.

"What's the meaning of this?" Palmer called over the clattering of the engine, drowning out the rippling moans from further down the hill and the incoming aircraft.

Kimberley jumped down from the driver's side as she left the engine running, and either hadn't heard or had simply ignored Palmer's protest.

"Clear everything out of the way!" she shouted, climbing back up into the cab without waiting for any response.

"Surely she's not trying to…" Palmer said, just as he saw Lloyd's face crack into an evil grin that bordered on madness, until his own mind tipped over into understanding.

"Clear the barricade," they both shouted in near unison, and watched as the men shoved and pulled at the furniture and crates providing them with the thinnest of barriers between supposed safety and a seemingly unstoppable onslaught of undead. Neither officer knew if the men understood the tenacious young woman's plan, but it only mattered that, at that very moment, they followed orders. When the roadway was sufficiently cleared, Lloyd called for them to stand clear, then held his left thumb up clearly in the light of the headlamps.

Inside the cab, Kimberley saw the gesture and did that curious, almost automatic action with her left hand of wiggling the gearstick to ensure it was in neutral, pointlessly as she wasn't depressing the clutch and the big, green truck was still idling and stationary. She leaned her right leg out of the open door in readiness and used both hands to depress the heavy button and release the handbrake, with her left foot wedged unnaturally on the middle pedal. The truck lurched slightly, creaking against the brakes as the pressure from her foot was less than that of the handbrake. She took two steadying breaths, her head rising up to see the oncoming horde a little over a hundred paces away, then rolled to her right and out onto the cobblestones.

The truck moved slowly at first, despite the pull of gravity. It's hulking green metal and canvas rolled slowly forwards as it began a journey that the laws of physics had already dictated. As certainly and as inescapably as fate, it rolled faster and faster by the second as it accelerated on a journey that would only end in devastation, but the devastation they wanted. As soon as it passed through the gap created in the barricade, orders were shouted for the hole to be sealed again and for the men to make ready. Kimberley ran to the barricade, slapping both hands onto an upturned sideboard as she watched, open-mouthed, at the rapidly retreating back end of the Bedford truck. The sheer bulk of the vehicle obscured the sight of it crashing headlong into the leading wave of the crowd.

She didn't see it, but she heard it. The soft, wet sounds of metal hitting flesh. The muted pops and crunches of sinew and bone giving way so terribly and inevitably under the onslaught of the tonnes of metal bearing down on them, crushing them, driving them into the roadway to be crushed and smeared as inconsequential sacks of meat, flinging them aside either whole or in parts until the resistance of so many hundreds of bodies adhered to those same inescapable laws of physics.

The truck slowed, still rolling downwards to crush and destroy the bodies as it went, until it burst from the other side of the crowd to slam into a single-storey building and all but collapse it on impact. The remains of the roof caved inwards, cascading tile and stones to the ground, and interrupting the instincts of the zombies at the rear.

Those mindless monsters, the ones following the others in

front with no understanding of why, were drawn to the noise and diverted from the main attack to mill about the nearest source of noise. At the head of their advance, those few not crushed by the hurtling truck, stomped onwards.

"Is it going to blow up?" a voice asked from behind the barricade as it broke the silence.

"No, lad," came the gruffly amused voice of Sergeant Hampton, "that's only in the mo…"

His retort was cut off by a double crump of explosions, making them all duck instinctively. Nervous eyes peered over the barricade to see a cloud of smoke where the blast had come from, just as the air above them tore with the ripping sounds of the helicopter passing low overhead.

It flared, spun on its axis, and exposed the open side door where the indomitable Squadron Sergeant Major stood with his feet firmly planted and murder in his eyes.

———

"Take us directly over them and go slow," Johnson had shouted into the headset he had been given by the loadmaster. A pause told him that either the pilot was deciding whether to do as he was asked, or that he was looking for the best way to approach the horde.

Johnson rummaged in the box held down by heavy canvas netting and came back with both hands full.

"Hold on to me," he shouted as he fixed Brinklow with a look and didn't wait for an answer. The loadmaster did as he was told and took a firm grip on the belt of his webbing as the big man leaned perilously close to falling out. Barrett slowed the aircraft from the flat-out speed he had forced it to on their return journey, just as Johnson saw the most unexpected event unfold below.

A Bedford truck, he had no idea whether it was being

driven in a fruitless escape attempt or not, gathered momentum as it rolled towards the attacking horde. His mouth dropped open as it slammed into the leading edge, obliterating the first dozen ranks of undead inside of a second as it ploughed through them mercilessly. His mouth stayed open, even if it did curl slightly into the very beginnings of a horrified smile, as the vehicle carried on throwing them down and crushing them as effectively as interlocking fire from heavy machine guns. He watched as the truck emerged from the far side of the horde to splay its headlight out from the grotesque shadows that had danced through the crowd, bursting into the relatively empty street behind their combined mass, only to slam into a building to bring it down. In the poor light below, Johnson saw the faint edges of the cloud of dust and steam caused by the crash and put his hands together to hook his thumbs into the release pins and pull them simultaneously.

Holding both hands as far out from the open fuselage door as he could, Johnson gauged the drop and distance so far as was possible in a split-second and opened both hands to drop the small bombs at what he hoped was the biggest concentration of dead left standing.

He didn't hear the double *whump* and crunch of the grenades exploding, as the hurtling aircraft was over them too fast for the sound to carry. His next glance down showed the ghostly outlines of upturned faces before the aircraft lurched and the wheels bumped to the ground to make him feel impossibly heavy on his feet. Staggering, he climbed down and reached back for the precious tools he had brought with him.

"Sergeant Major?" a nasal voice called from behind his turned back.

Johnson turned, hefting the long machine gun in one hand effortlessly and a box of linked ammunition in the other.

"Lieutenant," he acknowledged simply, no sound being heard over the engines but his mouth clearly making the word as he walked past the young officer and towards the barricade. Palmer was left standing under the wash of the spinning blades as the surge of civilians rushed towards the door. He switched on, counting them in and counting half a load. He fixed the loadmaster with a look until he was sure he had his attention, then held up a flat palm and told him to wait, mouthing the word carefully until he received a nod in reply.

Lieutenant Palmer ran to the barricade, placing a hand on Lloyd's shoulder to get his attention.

"Fifteen more on this load," he shouted, making the two officers and the SSM scan their lines. The numbers were evident. They would have to leave behind eight men.

"The other one is on its way," Johnson shouted, seeing instant confusion on the faces of the two men before his eyes flickered away to take in the sight of men without magazines in their guns.

"The other Sea King," he explained, "it's coming back in a few minutes."

The officers looked at each other before Lloyd spoke first.

"Leave me and my marines here, you get your lot gone."

Palmer seemed to bridle, as though the implication were that the marines were the superior soldiers and by definition braver. Then his chest deflated, and he looked expectantly, hopefully almost, up at the SSM.

"I need your medic and a few more back at the rendezvous. Feel free to stay with me, but I need a few of the best you have with me, and I need you to go back and look after what's left of our boys," he said in a tone that brokered no argument as he fixed the marine Lieutenant with a stare that spoke volumes.

It said that Johnson was, in no uncertain terms, ordering the Lieutenant back to base. It said that he wouldn't ask or even allow anyone else to stay in his place, and his firm grip on the GPMG solidified that intention. Lloyd held his eye for a moment longer and turned to speak to his sergeant. Johnson faced Palmer.

"Get the men without ammo on board," he instructed, "and get yourself back to the captain, Sir."

Palmer swallowed, nodded, and turned to do as he was told.

FOURTEEN

"Look alive," Johnson roared as he opened up with the big machine gun, firing short bursts as he swung the barrel left and right to target the closest groups of zombies. The arrival of the helicopter and the brief time it was nestled near the top of the island had served to encourage them all to renew their uphill journey, because they associated the noise with potential prey.

The harsh rattling, percussive hammering up close deafened the men, as a marine to his left focused on feeding the belt carefully into the weapon. Johnson knew they could ill afford a malfunction just then, when his unexpected arrival had quadrupled their firepower all by himself. When the first belt was about to run dry he let go of the trigger, feeling as well as hearing the sudden drop in noise, but imagining that the attack renewed in intensity as his gun went quiet. He knew that wasn't right, he knew that only a living enemy cowered in cover when in the sights of such a weapon, and these mindless, undead Screechers held no such regard for their own lives.

A slap on his shoulder told him that a fresh belt was seated, and he bent to the sights again and began hammering away at the remnants of the horde. When that second belt ran dry, he took his eyes away from the attack and glanced down at the box behind him, before flicking his gaze up to meet the eye of the staunch marine sergeant, to nod to him once.

That sergeant, Hampton, had stayed behind with five of his marines, all volunteers to a man, and included their sniper, who went about his own work methodically to line up two or more advancing heads, before squeezing the trigger and sending a fat, heavy round through their collective skulls.

Hampton hauled three of his men back from the barricade and began dishing out grenades like bottles of water on an aid mission. The marines, far more accustomed to the small bombs than their tank-driving counterparts, threw with ruthless efficiency to cut huge chunks out of the oncoming waves and fill the air with the crump and bang of explosions to punctuate the heavy rattle of gunfire.

The intensity of the noise was so extreme that the arrival of the second helicopter was felt before it was heard, as the rotor wash pushed them forward when it flared to land close behind them.

Johnson felt that arrival but could not afford to take his eyes from the enemy. The final belt of ammunition was slapped into his gun as he could feel the heat from the barrel radiating back to his face. Four hundred rounds had already been expended through it and his shoulder burned in pain with each squeeze of the trigger. He pulled it in tighter and carried on, deafened by his own personal destruction but yelling for the others to fall back. He felt another slap on his shoulder, this one telling him it was time to leave, and he stood a little taller to make his final stand.

The zombies were close by then, close enough to make out details of their uniforms and faces. He squeezed the trigger in one last surge as he bared his teeth and emitted a low growl of anger and frustration, firing an extended burst of fully automatic fire as he depressed and swung the long barrel left to right to left to spray the heavy bullets at the knees of the ranks of undead. His mind registered that they were thinning out, that he could not see heads of the fifth and sixth ranks of attackers, but there were still more bodies than bullets. When the gun finally ran dry he dropped it where he stood and turned to run towards the helicopter just as the barricade fell inwards under a wash of dead meat.

———

"There's a fight going on down there," Lieutenant

Commander Murray called into the headset to warn his four passengers, "I've got muzzle flashes and what looks like grenades."

Wordlessly, the four rear passengers unstrapped themselves and stood, holding on to whatever they could as they readied themselves to get back in the fight. All four of them, two bearded Special Boat Service troopers and the two Norwegian commandos of the FSK, were all on the edge of their nerves but what marked them out as special was their ability to compartmentalise. To forget their emotions and to focus on the task in hand. Both teams, originally four a piece, had been halved in brutal savagery only a few hours before, but the remaining men and woman vowed to not be so easily taken.

As the helicopter slowed and turned to present the open side door, the noise of heavy gunfire pounded them over the noise of the thudding blades and screaming engines. All four hopped to the ground and fanned out, two left and two right, in pairs of mixed teams.

Astrid dropped her right lower leg to the ground and rested her suppressed weapon on her left knee as she scanned for targets. The leader of the SBS team, the man even she had found herself calling Buffs, crouched over her with his weapon scanning in opposite arcs to her own.

Uniformed men ran towards them, empty handed or with useless rifles dangling on slings, and began to throw themselves on board the aircraft. A huge, rattling burst of automatic fire from a weapon far heavier than their own sub machine guns sounded ahead from the makeshift barricade and as soon as it stopped, Astrid saw a lone figure turn and sprint for them just as a wave of undead crushed the meagre obstacle to pour over it.

She was hauled to her feet and propelled towards the open door, but she spun with the force and brought her weapon back up to face the threat. Undetected except by the ones pulling their triggers, rounds spat with snapping coughs from their fat-barrelled guns to cut down the zombies regaining their feet and cover the man who ran straight towards them. As he slowed and began waving his arms at them to retreat, the sheer presence of the last man to fall back dominated the area. He grabbed them and pushed them inside before throwing himself bodily on top of the living bodies in the open doorway.

What the fuck are these idiots doing? Johnson thought to himself, incorrectly recognising the profiles of the four shooters as the SAS team he had sent to scout potential safe sites for them.

How did they even get on the helicopter? Came his next thought, before a shriek from behind him refocused his mind and forced him further on. A whip of wind passed his face, buffeting him almost imperceptibly under the downforce of the rotor blades and the dust and debris it sent towards his squinting eyes. Another half-felt sensation behind him made him stagger slightly as a flailing hand of a now-dead Screecher hit his leg as it tumbled to the roadway with two out of three bullets fired into its skull from the burst of one of the guns ahead of him. Slowing as much as he dared and roaring at them to get on the damned aircraft, he grabbed at their equipment and sent them hurtling towards safety before diving headlong on top of them and bawling at the top of his voice.

"Go! Fucking *go!*" he roared, feeling his body weight instantly tripled by the forces of gravity as the helicopter launched vertically skywards.

As he rolled to get to his knees, a slap of meat on metal made his eyes fix on a bloody hand gripping the ledge. Impossibly slowly, inch by terrifying inch, the top of a head rose to meet the hand and revealed the face beneath.

Despite the gore and blood, despite the missing right cheek exposing teeth all the way back to the molars and gouged-out left eye, Johnson came face to face with his missing radio operator, Corporal Mander. The former corporal hauled himself upwards, performing a one-handed chin-up of such epically strong proportions as to betray how the mind limits the body's ability. The ravaged mouth opened and leaned forward, making Johnson close his eyes and accept that he had nowhere to go.

A metallic clang sounded in front of his face, thudding the metal deck of the helicopter and vibrating his head painfully. He opened one eye to see the glinting head of an axe and four severed fingers. Following the head to the handle, his eyes matching the flowing contour of the wood and up the slender wrist and the forearm to see the concerned face of the young woman who had terrified him so much with her unexpected interest in him. She didn't smile, but her look of cold steel filled him with a warmth he suspected was rather unbecoming of a man of his position.

———

Corporal Mander went for the radio but found his path blocked by the tall and spare Major from the intelligence corps.

"I said we are to evacuate immediately," he hissed at him.

Mander ignored him, pushing past the man and going for the set on the desk. He had no time to explain to this man, who even though he was a reservist himself and not a full-time soldier, he saw as lower down on the food chain. Had a man like the captain given him an order, he would have followed it because he knew him to be a clever man who was tried and tested in battle; or even his Squadron Sergeant Major, who Mander saw much more of,

often being on the radio and pretending not to listen to the senior men of the squadron discussing matters.

If Mister Johnson had given the order to strip naked and do the hokey-kokey, then he would do precisely that.

But not this man. He snatched up the set and began to give a report over the channel he hoped his counterpart, Daniels, would be listening to in the Sultan out there somewhere, but after only a few words the door burst inwards.

Major Hadlington screamed foully, his high-pitched wails drowning out the entire upper spectrum of Mander's hearing as he went down to three of them. A noise behind him made him spin, amazing even himself that he could rip his eyes away from the officer being torn apart, and he saw the female radio operator who had relieved him. She was emerging from the door of the toilet near the radio desk and their eyes met and locked for a second. Saying nothing, he shoved her hard back inside and slammed the door just as a body fell on him from behind. Teeth ripped the skin from his face and lanced pain throughout his entire body as hot breath burned his eyes with the foul smell of salt water gone stagnant. His brain registered renewed screams, the same terrible high-pitched shrieking of impossible agony, and just as teeth gnawed at his right elbow and the lower part of the limb was torn sinuously away, his consciousness fled.

Minutes later, the former Corporal Mander woke, in as much as his reanimated body opened its milky eyes and pushed itself one-handedly off the blood-drenched floor. Three others were in the room with him, not that he recognised them, and the thing they fed on didn't smell fresh to him. He heard noises from outside, from beyond the door left hanging open, and he stumbled his way through it. Outside in the cool, dark air he lifted his chin and sniffed deeply, turning his face left and up to where the sounds of gunfire echoed from past the huge crowd of the others like him.

Shortly after that, a huge green truck rocketed past him, the oversized wing mirror clipping his shoulder hard enough to break it in two places and spin him around to land hard on the cobbles. He righted himself again and re-orientated towards the renewed sounds of heavier gunfire. His long, halting stumble uphill was sparked by the thudding sounds of a huge machine which started to move as he approached. Clamping his one remaining hand onto the lip of the open door he hauled himself upwards to be rewarded instantly with the smell of fresh meat. He opened his mouth, savouring the delights to come, and was suddenly in mid-air and falling back towards the ground where he had started. The smell of meat vanished, and his remaining senses blacked out in a heartbeat as his skull burst on impact to spill his brains onto the roadway.

CHAPTER

FIFTEEN

Barrett slammed his aircraft down to the dark ground, his entire body fatigued with the physical effort of piloting the big helicopter for over an hour of intensive short hops under immense pressure.

Real, literal, life and death pressure.

He waited until given the all-clear from his loadmaster, signifying that everyone was off, and he moved his helicopter to the flat area adjacent to their landing spot; hovering it just a few feet off the ground as the tall beast crabbed sideways.

"Julian? Julian?" a nasal voice called out, snapping Captain Palmer's attention directly to the unnecessary source of the noise. Mixed relief and annoyance washed over him, and he stepped straight to his younger brother and hushed him, if anything for the embarrassment of the men seeing their officers engaging in such an emotional reunion.

"Lieutenant," he snapped, sending the message loud and clear which they both heard in their late father's voice.

Stop your caterwauling! He cried from the depths of their shared childhood, *you're neither women nor animals; show some decorum.*

Second-Lieutenant Palmer stopped, wiped the look from his face and resisted the urge to hug his big brother and not let go.

"Sir," he said formally, finally, "I'm glad you're safe."

"Where's the SSM?" his older brother fired back, seemingly unaffected by the emotion of their being reunited. Palmer junior swallowed down the first four things he wanted to say, settling on a brief but thorough report.

"He stayed behind, waiting for the other aircraft and in command of the final group."

"I see," the captain said, dropping his eyes in thought. Without another word he thrust a pad and pencil into his younger brother's chest and waited for him to take them.

"I've begun taking a record of who we have left. Unless there are any surviving members of Assault Troop left behind, I'd suggest you start with Sergeant Sinclair's men."

The younger Palmer, left without the emotional response to his survival that he had hoped for and, worse still, unrecognised for the fact that he had finally led fighting men in contact and done what he felt was a good job. The final nail in the coffin of his elation was seeing his brother, the man he idolised and tried to emulate all the time, physically grab hold of another officer and turn him to walk away.

"Chris," he said, using Lieutenant Lloyd's first name in a rare display of familiarity, "with me, if you please."

Second Lieutenant Palmer sneered, almost crushing the pad in his hand and digging the dull point of the pencil into his flesh painfully, then stomped away to take the most uncaring and callous butcher's report ever.

Nestling the aircraft gently back to the ground, Barrett flicked the switches to kill the big jet engines and sank into his seat in pure physical and psychological relief. Pulling off the helmet and headset, he basked in the sudden, if only relative, silence.

That silence was shattered by the shouting of a polite enquiry, even if the voice calling out was filled with tension and authority.

"I say?" the voice called again, "where are the others?"

"I'll deal with this, Harry," his co-pilot said as he pulled himself from his seat far faster than his slightly older comrade, "you take a moment."

"Thank you, James," Barrett said tiredly to Morris in an unusually intimate moment where the two men used each other's given names, similar to the conversation that had just occurred

two dozen paces away.

"Ah, Captain," Barrett heard Morris exclaim from behind him as he leaned back and closed his eyes briefly.

"Lieutenant," Captain Palmer said as formally as his rushed mood allowed, "might I enquire where the rest are?"

"Yes, Captain," Morris said with a groan as he climbed down, "the other aircraft by my reckoning should be roughly six minutes behind us, all being well."

"All being well?" Palmer asked pointedly.

"Well, yes," Morris replied, fighting the urge to recite no less than two film references given the evident seriousness of the question, "the Sergeant Major was rather heroically taking on an entire horde of undead when we left," he said, hurrying to add his next sentence, given the widening eyes on the face of the army captain, "but he was far from alone; he had marines and some of your men around him and they were fighting hard."

"And the other helicopter?" Palmer asked.

"Got released from command to return, I presume," Morris said, leaving the explanation for Lieutenant Commander Murray's return flight for the pilot himself, "they should have collected and been in the air by now," he finished.

Palmer nodded, the gesture unseen in the poor light and

adding a verbal acknowledgement hurriedly, and turned away to wait for the tell-tale sounds of the other helicopter coming in.

———

"Head count," Johnson shouted as he shakily regained his feet. The sound of his voice was snatched away in the massive drone of the jet engines and the thudding blades. A headset appeared on his chest, held out by a lean, blonde woman he did not recognise. He knew instantly that she did not belong as part of their civilian complement, given her clothing and equipment, but similarly couldn't place her or understand how she came to be there.

Pulling on the headphones and adjusting the boom microphone, he untangled himself from the long spiral cable snaking upwards. As he did so, his eyes took in three other forms in similar clothing and carrying weapons he hadn't seen for real outside of anti-terrorism displays, marking out the four of them as special forces, and he half recognised the brooding, bearded man to his left as one of the SBS team who went out on that very helicopter.

"Report," he said.

"There was an outbreak on the ship," said the bearded man, not adding a 'sir' or other appropriate deference, which all but announced his specialist status, "they sank it just after we took off. The whole fleet is pulling back, and they've fired nukes on Russia because Russia apparently launched nukes on Europe."

All of this information, although garnered from different sources, slotted in with what the SSM already knew. He glanced around the others in the dull, red-lit interior, seeing the filthy and exhausted faces of men, of soldiers and marines, who had fought hard right down to their last bullet. Of men who had gone toe-to-toe with the Screechers and taken the fight to them with the bayonet. Of men who had gone to the brink of survival and still couldn't believe that they had got away with it. Johnson looked at those faces, counting thirteen including the four mysterious passengers already on board, and watched in sudden terror as every one of their eyes went wide.

Lieutenant Commander Murray, staying quiet and concentrating hard after the adrenaline of the rapid landing and take-off, headed inland at speed. As he levelled out the angle of attack, flattening the aircraft to cruise, his hand slipped on the throttle and slowed the aircraft. His grip on the cyclic was shaky, his palm seemingly sweaty, but the myriad smells inside the helicopter masked the metallic tang of fresh blood where the wound in his arm had opened up once more. So intense was his concentration that he missed the signs until they were too late, and as the aircraft slowed more and more, his foggy brain, left weak and confused by the blood loss, registered the warning too late.

The unbending laws of physics, that point where gravity outweighed lift, kicked in hard and the bulbous, ungainly helicopter dropped like a stone. As the momentary weightlessness made the eyes of all the passengers bulge, Johnson was pitched over to land hard, flat on his back. His eyes registered a handful of others in similar positions as another weird sense tugged his insides backwards through his spine, as the aircraft's tail whipped around to overtake the cockpit and eject two men from the open side door and into the night air.

It was that last second spin of the fuselage, combined with the lucky position he had fallen in, that made the difference between survival and death to Johnson. As the tail of the craft hit the main part of the church, which was the only tall feature in an otherwise unremarkable countryside village, the belly of the helicopter slammed into the ground hard. So hard, in fact, that the two people who had somehow managed to stay standing were flattened into the deck on impact like meat concertinas. The severe spinal injuries alone would have killed them, but the worst were the ones who were neither lucky enough to be in positions to survive the crash, nor to be killed in an instant.

One man, a marine, was on his knees after the lurching change of direction had spilled him forwards. As the belly of the aircraft hit the ground his face was pitched forward so violently to meet the upcoming rush of the metal deck that his face flattened, and the contents of his shattered skull pulped into a foul ooze that sprayed instantly out in all directions, as if a grenade had detonated inside his head.

Another was only halfway falling when they struck the ground. There was an eruption of bright, white bone from his shoulder as the straight, bracing arm forced the flesh outwards, until the force ripped the entire shoulder off, to pour thick, hot blood in great gouts over the deck.

Johnson stared at a face opposite where he lay, his ears screaming with the tortured noises, and his head pounding. He was both soaked with the blood of others and sprayed with so many different fluids from the injuries that he felt like a modern art project.

The face, remarkably unblemished if still very dirty, looked at him with pure disbelief and shock. The eyes were wide, the eyebrows slightly lifted and the mouth open to complete the look. Johnson found his eyes staring straight ahead at the chin of the face, scanning downwards towards his own toes, to see the lifeless eyes in more detail, then back up to where the view made him pause for a few heartbeats, until he finally under-stood what was wrong. The man's head appeared to be on backwards to his body, and the oddly twisted folds of skin around his neck under his ears told the story of how he had somehow had his head twisted backwards in the crash.

As the sounds of dying metal faded, Johnson's eyes closed a

fraction more with every laboured outward breath, until the darkness ever so subtly overcame him.

―――――

Peter, unable to sleep because of the sporadic noises far off in the dark night, sat on the kitchen worktop in silence and waited, straining to hear what he thought had been a helicopter. He had long ago conquered the normal childish fears of the dark, having been forced to sit in pitch-black woodland by his father until he had stopped crying and started listening.

Nothing can creep up on you in the dark, his father had told him, *not if you listen properly.* Despite the valuable lesson so heartlessly delivered, Peter knew with utter certainty that there were in fact things that could creep up on him in the dark, and they frightened him even more than the memory of his father.

He had crept back upstairs twice to check on Amber, finding her in a different position each time, but always with the threadbare stuffed lamb clutched to her body, and the cat somewhere on or next to her, curled into a tight ball.

Now, just when those far-off sounds faded into nothing, he slipped down from the kitchen side to land silently on the tiled floor in his new socks, which had been liberated from the bedside drawers of the former occupant, and which were evidently too large for his small feet.

As he reached out to shut the small window, since the cat had now decided that it had enjoyed enough fun roaming the countryside, and had come back inside to settle, another sound pricked the very edge of his hearing. Instinctively opening his mouth and turning his head to the side to allow for better hearing, he heard a mechanical noise which his young brain automatically associated with the word *falling*.

Sure enough, the spinning, almost Doppler-effect sound was answered by a single loud crash. Peter hesitated, then shut the window quietly and climbed the stairs with deliberate placement of his feet to move noiselessly, as had become his first instinct.

Creeping to the draw curtains at the large master bedroom overlooking the road, Peter inched back the edge of the curtain so as not to make any movement that might attract unwelcome attention. He scanned the skyline over the barely discernible rooftops of the few scattered houses on the opposite side of the single road running through the village. Cutting up each section of what he thought was the horizon into small sections, and looking carefully at them one by one, he could see no evidence of anything he was expecting.

He had to admit to himself that he didn't really know what he was expecting, but he hoped that he would recognise it when he saw it. With the front aspect giving him nothing, he gently lowered the curtain and walked silently to the rooms at the rear with the largest windows offering what would be stunning panoramic views in sunlight. Still being careful to move the curtains slowly, he was more confident that looking out of the rear was safer, because it looked out directly onto the low-rolling fields instead of the roads and houses on the opposite side. Still he could make out nothing.

Unable to come up with any further options that didn't involve going outside in the dead of night, he decided that his curiosity would have to wait until daybreak, and he crept back to where Amber slept, to settle down on his own bed beside her.

CHAPTER

SIXTEEN

"They're late," Lloyd offered pointlessly.

"So it would appear…" Palmer responded in an almost distant voice as his head was turned upwards to the night sky. Their reverie was interrupted by Corporal Daniels, who was calling the captain's name in a voice that bordered on the too loud, given their tenuous situation.

"Here," Palmer responded, knowing that the man clearly had something important to say, hearing the insistence in his voice.

"Sir," he began as he leaned in to prevent their voices from carrying too far, which was odd since they were hoping to expect a helicopter to arrive and land there soon, "word from Charlie-One-One. They've scouted one of the options now and are happy that we can defend it if we need to."

"Excellent," Palmer answered, "which one?"

"It's actually not on the list, Sir, but they came across a sign for it and decided it was worth a flutter."

"What is it then?"

"Some kind of historical country estate, Sir," Daniels told

him, summing up all that he knew of this place in his next sentence.

"It's mostly got a wall around it, but there are weak points they can strengthen with vehicles and obstacles."

"Sounds like my cup of tea," Palmer said casually, as he could almost hear the cogs turning in the brain of this radio man who seemed to take everything literally. That trait made him entertaining when drinking, but less so in high-stress combat situations where a metaphor is used casually.

"How far away, Corporal?" Palmer asked before the next question wasted precious time.

"Roughly forty minutes by road as long as we don't have too many detours, Sir," Daniels responded.

"Thank you, Corporal. Anything else of note mentioned?"

"No, Sir," Daniels said.

"Very well. Mister Lloyd, will you kindly speak to Sergeant Maxwell and see to it that we find sufficient transport for everyone?"

Lloyd's boots answered for him as he set off towards the large building they had occupied, with a muttered, "Sir," as he went.

"Daniels, stay on the radio and see if you can find someone to refuel our Spartan."

"Yes, Sir," Daniels answered, turning to leave before he hesitated, and half turned back.

"Sir?" he enquired.

"I shall be here, Corporal," he said in a resigned voice, "waiting for the helicopter's imminent arrival. On that note, kindly send me the first man you see to act as a runner. Thank you, Corporal," he finished, dismissing the man, who did as he was told, grabbing a pair of troopers who were walking nearby and passing on the captain's orders.

"Here, Sir," said Trooper McGill from Sergeant Strauss'

One Troop as he approached the darker silhouette of the officer. "You needed a runner?"

"Yes, both of you to the other aircraft and pass on this message: attempt radio contact with second helicopter, send update to me directly," he said, affecting a more formal, almost robotic tone for the wording of the order, before adding, "then one of you remain and wait for news whilst the other returns to me for other orders."

"Yes, Sir," McGill answered, intending to come back himself, despite the two of them having just been rotated out for a short break to eat and rest.

"Now," Palmer muttered under his breath, as the unexpected delay was beginning to cause him more than a little anxiety with each minute that ticked past, "where the devil are you?"

————

Johnson's eyes flickered open, his brain not understanding but his instincts kicking in as a response to the intense heat he felt. The outbreak of a fire somewhere inside the fuselage was threatening to consume the surviving helicopter passengers with smoke and heat before the flames burst out to devour anything left behind.

Groaning and turning in agony to rise unsteadily onto all fours, Johnson took one long, deep breath in and vomited hard onto the hot metal deck under his face. Gasping and gagging for air, he repeated the process twice until he had totally voided his stomach, which he hadn't realised was still so full. He couldn't remember when he had last eaten, but he knew from the semi-digested smell that it must have been some time ago.

"Any..." he tried to call out, coughing hard to prompt another dry retch and a nauseating belch with it. He cleared his throat and tried again, this time emitting a cracking, rasping, hoarse whisper.

"Anyone alive?" he called out, earning a groan from his left where a hand fluttered from beneath the uniform of a marine with a broken body. He reached out, grabbing the hand and was in the process of trying to haul it towards himself when a much stronger grip clamped on to the shoulder straps of his webbing and began to shunt him backwards in jerky movements. His right hand fumbled numbly as he cried out with an unintelligible moan of fear and anger, and, almost drunkenly, he worked the stiff leather strap away from the handle on the front of his webbing until the bayonet slid out uncertainly into his hand. He began to thrust it weakly upwards at the face and head behind him, striking out blindly in a desperate attempt to save himself from being eaten alive.

"Oi," came a simple answer rich with annoyance and impatience, "mind sticking that fucking thing somewhere else?"

Johnson, as though alcohol had dulled his wits, couldn't understand why this zombie had the power of speech or what new manner of hell he was experiencing. He even wondered for a brief moment whether he was alive at all, or conscious, or whether what was happening to him now was simply his imagination providing him with yet another nightmare to endure.

He didn't respond to the request and continued to jab upwards with grunts of effort, as he stabbed until he felt his body weight drop suddenly, and his wrist was grabbed. The bayonet was prised from his fingers and the voice sounded in his muffled brain once more.

"It's alright, I've got you," it said in a voice that might have been meant to be soothing, "I've got you."

Johnson didn't quit, but his mind and body retreated. They let him down, and he was forced to submit to being disarmed and dragged backwards out of the helicopter and onto damp grass, with the last thing he saw from inside being the fluttering hand gaining flat purchase on the deck to push upwards. The smells and other stimuli around him still got through, but it was as though he was conscious in a coma and aware of everything around him, yet unable to break the barrier and communicate.

He was propped with his back against a tree and had a weapon rested in his lap. His numb hands twitched as though he wanted to pick it up, to drop out the magazine and check for brass, then reload and make the weapon ready to fight, but nothing happened. His head lolled to the side, and he was forced to watch in silence as the shape which had dragged him out went back to the helicopter to be silhouetted against the dull light coming from inside it. That shape returned again and again, each time dragging another person out of the wreckage until his last return journey showed only an armful of equipment. He didn't make another trip back inside but returned to where he had placed Johnson and four others.

Johnson's wits slowly returned, and he became aware of new sounds and sensations. He could hear and feel his breath again and he could now smell the acrid smoke and see the first flickers of orange light coming from the fuselage to make the shadows dance. That smoke was laced with the indescribable tinge of plastic, which made his ever-increasingly alert brain register stimuli with knowledge.

Electrical fire, he told himself as he connected the dots, *probably a short in a wiring loom.*

Whether he was right or not made no difference to him, he was just happy that his brain was beginning to function again and the ringing in his ears was fading. With that torturous white noise dissipating, a crack of a twig in the undergrowth made his head whip to his left, causing sudden pain all down his body, although the instinctive movement of his hands made him feel reassured. He had grabbed up the Sterling sub machine gun and pointed it waveringly in the direction of the unexpected sound, only to wait for nothing to happen.

Couldn't be a Screecher, he told himself, *not even the fast ones would hold off on an attack. Must be an animal. That's right, just an animal.*

He jumped in fright as he failed to detect the approach of someone from in front of him, and he found himself looking into the pale face of the woman he hadn't recognised from the flight out. Up close he saw that she had long facial features and wide, pale eyes. His assumption that she didn't seem to be a Brit was confirmed when she spoke to him.

"Do you have any pain in your neck?" she asked in accented English with and undulating quality to the rhythm of her words. He shook his head, deciding that 'pain' by his measure was something that stopped him working.

"Any double vision or spots in front of your eyes?" she asked as she shone a painfully bright light into his face.

"No," he grumbled, pushed further into consciousness by the light which now left him night-blind, "how many?" he asked, meaning to get the number of survivors, but already having a terribly low figure in his head.

"Six," she said, devastating him with the news of over two-thirds of the bravest men lost. Johnson grimaced, and began the laborious process of struggling to his feet. The woman helped him, watching him like a hawk as he rested for a long time with one hand on the tree trunk and the other cradling the weapon as he rested it on his knee. Eventually he righted himself, and the woman told him she had to check on the others and left without another word. The SSM's vision returned slowly, and he used the trick of not looking directly at something in the dark to try and see the shapes with the edge of his eye. It worked to a degree and he could see a taller man helping a shorter one walk. The shorter man tried to wave him away and pushed on with a pronounced limp which made him only place his right foot on the ground for the shortest possible time. He didn't last long doing this, and he dropped to the ground again, cursing. Johnson staggered towards him, seeing the other man who was helping morph out of the shadows to become the SBS team commander.

"Go see to the others," Johnson told him, "I'll deal with this."

The bearded man left without saying anything else, disappearing into the gloom to leave the SSM looking down at the Royal Marine Sergeant. He couldn't recall the man's name but knew him to be a good, reliable man. He was also lucky, evidently, and tough.

"Ankle?" Johnson asked him as he knelt heavily beside him.

"Knee," the sergeant gasped through gritted teeth, "bent the fucker backwards when I landed. Popped straight back in but it's knackered."

Johnson fumbled with his pouches trying to find anything to strap the man up with, finding only the clotting trauma bandage given to him when they first deployed with weapons. Wrapping it tightly around the knee and hearing the controlled intakes of breath through the muted growls of the injured man he tied off the bandage tightly without twisting the built-in tourniquet too tightly. The man reached into his own pouches and passed another one to the SSM.

"Stick another one 'round it," he said breathlessly, "high and low. Keep the joint straight. I'm Bill Hampton, by the way."

Johnson did as he was asked, nodding as he remembered the man's name the second he had said it, immobilising the joint to prevent the damage from worsening and the pain from debilitating him. When he was done the Sergeant held up a hand and Johnson looked at it briefly before hauling him to his feet. The curious walk the sergeant stomped off performing would have been hilarious to watch in any other circumstances, as he hopped forward with his left foot, before swinging the straight right leg around in a low swoop to propel him forward again. The man must have been in incredible pain, but his resolve burned through as he stooped awkwardly to retrieve a weapon from the pile of salvaged equipment. Righting himself and inspecting the action of the SA80 rifle, he looked around and chose a defensive position where he could lean on the low graveyard wall to defend the crash site.

"Enfield," he called out softly, "with me, lad."

Johnson was startled again, evidence of just how dulled his senses had become because of the crash, as a tall man moved past him in an almost ghostly way. The man had a long rifle on his back, strapped diagonally, but he also stopped to retrieve a weapon from the pile and moved to take up the position with his sergeant.

A raised voice off to his left made him turn back, dizzying himself again with the regretfully fast movement of his head. He saw the blonde woman kneeling beside the bearded man over another figure and heard that same accented, undulating voice.

"Can you hear me? Open your eyes for me?" she said loudly.

"It's no good," the bearded man said as Johnson approached, "she's out cold."

"Who is i…" Johnson started to say before his eyes took in the unconscious woman with the livid cut to her scalp which had sheeted the right side of her face in blood.

"Kimberley!" he blurted out, "Miss Perkins," he added, even now conscious of the looks he would be receiving in the dark.

"We need to get out of here," the bearded man said as he rose, "every dead fucker inside of five miles would have heard that come down and every other dead fucker will come this way when that fire takes off for good," he grumbled as he turned to face the SSM, "Bufford. Sergeant, Boat Service," he said by way of introduction.

"Johnson. SSM, Yeomanry," the taller man replied. The two shook hands briefly in the growing light from the flames in the near distance.

"I can carry her," Bufford said, "can you walk okay? Use a weapon?"

"Yes," Johnson answered both questions with a single word, "where to?"

"No idea. Pilot bought it on impact and I don't know the area or the objective."

"Objective is the armour camp," Johnson told him, "and I do know the area. Give me a second," he said as he walked unsteadily away towards the church. Returning a few seconds later he announced, "Saint Goswald's."

"And where's that?" Bufford asked.

"Bad news, it's about twenty miles off course," Johnson answered, "we're at least twelve as the crow flies from the camp, and overland at night gives us no chance of making it today."

"Comms?" Bufford asked.

In answer Johnson turned to look at the helicopter which now burned against the church to light the area. The three of them paused in silence for a moment, then as though some silent signal had been received in all of their brains at once, they adjusted their equipment and readied themselves for a long, tense walk. Bufford bent and picked up the woman to cradle her in his arms and the rest of the weapons were doled out, with the foreign female holding out one of the suppressed weapons to Johnson. He took it, but her grip on the weapon didn't release.

"It belonged to my friend," was all she said, then turned away to take her place in the slow-moving line of people.

CHAPTER

SEVENTEEN

Daybreak saw Captain Palmer with red-rimmed eyes still looking up at the skies in the forlorn hope that a helicopter would magically appear and solve all of his worries.

The butcher's bill he had asked for had resulted in a total of a little over forty men remaining and as many civilians. They had rescued marines and troopers alike, but as yet, none of the men with scarlet berets had been accounted for. Hearing the piecemeal accounts of the battle on the island made him realise that the fiercest fight would have been at the low ground where all of the Royal Military Police had been posted. The most interesting of those accounts came from the Royal Marine Lieutenant who had given his report in a flat monotone with distant eyes.

He had said how his collection of men had been losing the battle for the beachhead, and when he'd realised that there were infected running around in the rear, he'd abandoned the fight to make it uphill and collected people wherever they could. The way he described his loose formation made Palmer think of older battles where infantry found themselves caught in the open by cavalry, and they contracted to form a rally square and defend themselves against the men on horseback who could cut down a fleeing man with laughable ease. That loose formation, horribly clear in the captain's mind, crab-crawled its way up the steep cobbles, until Lloyd joined the defence of the helicopter landing with the captain's younger brother. Palmer wanted to ask how the Second-Lieutenant had performed, had wanted some reassurance that he shouldn't be ashamed of how much the men disliked him, and that, when the chips were down, he had stepped up to the mark and become a leader.

He was too polite to ask outright, so waited for mention of him in Lloyd's report. The marine had said how he had joined the defence, not assumed command of it, and that reassured him

somewhat that the family name wasn't tainted with a useless soldier.

The stories of that defence came from different sources, all of which spoke of desperation and the relief that came with the arrival of the big Sergeant Major, who laid down a thunderous fire from the weapon he had been handed just before he took off. The scramble of the civilians to get away, the arrival of the ebullient, if not questionably senile Colonel Tim, who recreated the tales of how he had slain the enemy with his family's claymore, utterly failing to understand that the *enemy* of which he spoke had been former friends and comrades of those he recited his heroic deeds to. As always, the two privates charged with his protection and general babysitting stood behind him, wearing blank expressions of apology for what they were hearing.

Sometime in the night, long after the runner he had released to his other duties had returned to say that, try as they might, the other helicopter crew simply was not responding to any of their hails, Palmer had turned to more practical matters and focused on organising food, water and transport for the survivors and turned his mind towards the immediate matters.

"Sergeant Maxwell?" he called as he walked towards the huddle of men planning around a map.

"Sir," the sergeant said as he stood.

"A word, if you please, Sergeant," Palmer said, retreating a few steps back from the others.

"Mister Johnson hasn't returned, as I'm sure you are aware," he said in a soft voice.

"No, Sir," Maxwell replied, in a voice laced with anger and regret.

"You will assume his duties for now as senior NCO," Palmer told him, "I've discussed the matter with Lieutenant Lloyd and he is in agreement that we form the men differently. We don't have the numbers to operate as an armoured unit, nor do we have the

machinery or firepower."

"About that, Sir," Maxwell said, his face showing no excitement or pride at his field promotion, as he genuinely felt no excitement or pride in having to replace a man he respected, "I think it's possible to get through the camp to fetch more wagons and ammo for them."

"Do tell," Palmer prompted him.

"See, Sir," Maxwell explained, "we've landed in the opposite side to where we started, before you joined us, I mean, and we could cross the training grounds in the middle to get to the other entrance. We can pick up more wagons there, hopefully fuel them and come out to where the ammo dump is. We can meet up at the place the others have found then."

Palmer paused to think about it for a moment, one finger tapping at his lips.

"Very well," he finally agreed, "but not you. Sergeant Sinclair can take a dozen men, and make sure that chap who

Mister Johnson had a dislike for is attached. Unless you think that's unwise?"

"Nevin, Sir? I'll make sure he's on that, don't you worry," Maxwell assured him, taking to his senior NCO role naturally, "I'll see to it. When do you want to move out?"

"As soon as possible, I'd say," Palmer told him, "get these civilians somewhere that they can get some proper rest and something to eat. Speaking of that, the rations?"

"Plenty of rat-packs, Captain. Reckon we will probably need two trips to get people and supplies sorted," he explained, cursing the unusual lack of large transport trucks found by the dozen in such camps, "but I dare say the helicopter can take a good few of the people or supplies."

Palmer thought again, tapping his lip with the tip of his forefinger once more before he turned and called the marine Lieutenant over. Lloyd joined them at a jog, despite being only a

half-dozen paces away.

"All civilians, equipment and rations to be loaded on board the available transports and the helicopter. Discuss with Lieutenant Commander Barrett which he believes is best to go on board their aircraft; heavy rations or people," he said to Lloyd before turning back to Maxwell. "Get Sinclair to pick his men, make sure Trooper Nevin is included, and discuss your plan with him before bringing it to me."

Both men accepted their orders and went about it as Palmer walked away preparing to smooth their resident senior officer into condoning their plans. Finding the man with his feet up and a tin mug of something hot nestled in his hands, he switched on every drop of aristocratic charm and made his approach.

"Colonel," he greeted the man warmly, "I trust you are well?"

"Captain...?" the colonel said as he made a silent gesture of snapping his fingers before his face.

"Palmer, Sir," Palmer said with a hint of a bow in deference to the man. The gesture pleased the colonel, evidently, as he slapped his thigh.

"Palmer, yes, yes, of course. Sit down, man. You must be positively exhausted," he finished, leaving Palmer unsure as to whether it was a question or a statement, so pitching his response at an equally ambiguous level.

"Quite," he said with all the upper-class mannerism he could affect, "the thing is, Sir, I've rather got my hands full with the more mundane matters and we could do with you taking the lead on something, if I could be so bold as to impose?"

"Tell me, Captain," the colonel said as he leaned forward in his chair and lowered one arthritic leg to the ground at a time, "supply raid? Attack on an enemy stronghold? Speak, man!"

"Nothing quite so strenuous, I'm afraid," Palmer responded with a winning smile and a chuckle, "it's more that I need someone to spearhead our move to the other location; somewhere

far better suited to our style, I might add," he finished with a rueful look.

"I'm your man, Captain," he said as he stood and rubbed his hands together, "and Captain?"

"Sir?"

"I appreciate we are in the field, but a shave and some appropriate headgear will make all the difference to the men," the colonel said, reminding Palmer that the man was quite out of touch with reality.

"Yes, Sir," he said, "I shall do my best."

————

Amber awoke not long after the sunlight shone straight beams through the small gaps in the curtains. Peter was awake, having only napped on and off throughout the rest of the night after he had searched for what he suspected was a crashed heli-copter. Leaving her before she woke, he went to the upper windows again and this time made out a thin pillar of oily smoke behind them over a low rise. Chewing his lip as the distance was much further than he'd imagined, he went back downstairs and poured himself more water before opening the window, ready for the cat to leave for the day, and then went back to their room to sit on his bed and think before Amber finally stirred and displaced the tight coil of dirty fur.

The cat woke, unfolding itself like a snake emerging from a pot, and stood on all four paws to arch its back upwards in an upside-down U as it tensed and held its tail out stiffly behind it. As lazily as it started, the stretch ended suddenly as the cat sat back with lightning speed and stuck out a hind leg to lick at the outstretched limb.

"Hello," said a small voice, making Peter's heart skip, as Amber had spoken once more. He opened his mouth to respond but stopped himself from making any sound as he watched her reach out and fuss the cat, seeing it slink back-wards and forwards past her hand to ensure that both sides of its face were adequately rubbed against her.

Again, with no indication, the cat stepped lightly off her bed and trotted from the room with its tail held high and curled over at the end.

"It's like a question mark," Peter said softly, turning to look at Amber who rubbed her sleepy eyes and asked him a ques-tion with her tilted head.

"His tail. He curls it over like a question mark at the end."

She shrugged, as though the observation was pointless to her, but conveyed no annoyance at him speaking. She climbed out of bed, hair a mess, and tucked the stuffed lamb that Peter had given her back into bed. He couldn't help but smile as she arranged the duvet nicely over it, ensuring it was smooth and that the lamb was comfortable.

She walked out of the room, wavering from side to side as she hadn't fully regained her alertness, and he heard her shut the door to the bathroom. Peter had taken the precaution, as unpleasant as it was, of placing a small bucket inside the bowl so that the flush wouldn't serve as a dinner bell and attract anyone or anything to their presence. He planned to take the bucket into the secluded back garden and pour the contents into the brook which ran past, the same one that would still hold traces of the bloated, rotting corpse he had killed. The theory of this worked fine, and he had been forced to do something similar in his past when he and his sister had been banned from using the taps or flushing the toilets.

He waited in the room, planning to let her go downstairs before he added his own waste to the bucket to take it straight outside. The bucket would then go into the downstairs toilet off the kitchen for them to use throughout the day.

He had plans for them, and with it looking likely to be a hot day, he was hoping to get started soon before the sun got higher in the sky. His thoughts of what to do, namely emptying, clearing out and marking the nearest houses before shutting them up tight to prevent anything getting inside them, were interrupted by a shout.

It was Amber, clearly, but the shout was more of an open-mouthed grunt. He flew from his bed and raced towards the bathroom, the spike he had fashioned already in his hand, but instead saw her standing in the doorway, beckoning him frantically towards her. He ran, his loose socks bunching up on his feet as they caught in the thick carpet of the landing as he covered the short distance to her. He didn't know why, but his protective urges with her ran so deep that his body responded without his mind making a choice. Before he reached her, she skipped back inside and climbed up onto the side of the bath to lean on the sink and shoot a hand out straight ahead of her, extending a finger out of the window.

Peter's gaze started at her shoulder, following down her small arm and stared past the pointing digit to the daylight outside. Neither of them moved, and neither of them breathed as they watched a line of shapes advancing slowly. Peter's heart dropped, having never expected to face the dead coming from the unexpected side across the brook from the fields beyond.

As he looked, and as his brain began to register something wrong, or at least the absence of something wrong, it finally dawned on him that the line of people walking their way weren't dead.

And that frightened him more.

CHAPTER

EIGHTEEN

"Hold up," Johnson said exhaustedly, as he nodded his head behind him at the stiff-legged sergeant Hampton, who offered no argument, "he needs to rest."

The man he had called, the bearded SBS sergeant, said nothing but simply pointed to the hedge line ahead, indicating the nearest cover. Reaching it first and scanning left and right, he caught the eye of the blonde woman and pointed her to his left as he went off to the right.

Pushing out a perimeter, Johnson thought as his brain gave commentary on everything. He could barely think as he put his effort into carrying the dead weight of the woman he was trying not to look down at. Every time he did, he missed his footing and staggered off sideways instead of concentrating on making forward progress over the uneven ground. Three of them had taken turns at carrying Kimberley, the injured Hampton and the small-statured Astrid Larsen being excused the responsibility. They trudged and traipsed their way across country, twice struggling to find breaks in the dark and having to track sideways to find a style or a gate to get through the thick hedgerows. They had to pass Kimberley over hand to hand, seeing as the blow to her head kept her unconscious throughout. Then they climbed over themselves, their actions punctuated by some of the most colourfully bad language any of them had ever heard coming from the mouth of sergeant Hampton. Kimberley, being unconscious, escaped the experience and the sniper, Enfield, had heard it all before. But the others, even the experienced and irascible Johnson and the SBS man, turned an eyebrow up at it.

Astrid, despite her strong grip on the English language, misunderstood most of what he said and struggled to find any logical sense in the way he combined religion with farm poultry.

Resting Kimberley gently onto the ground and arranging her into something resembling a recovery position, Johnson slumped beside her and caught his breath for a few moments.

"Village ahead," Enfield said, peering through the scope of his big rifle, "can only see the rear of these houses, but there are rooftops, behind which means more houses opposite. Another church, too," he finished, stating the obvious as the short spire was the tallest feature ahead of them.

"Jesus tit-wanking fucking Christ," Hampton blasphemed in a foul hiss of words as he lowered himself as close to the ground as possible before submitting to gravity and slumping down the rest of the way to land heavily and spark off the string of obscenities.

Bufford trotted back to them, stopping at speaking distance and dropping to one knee with his back to them, and scanning the open countryside with a relative air of relaxation. He knew that he'd have plenty of time to react should any of them discover their ragged group in the open. Seeing that the bearded man had returned, or *contracted* as her own word would have translated, she mirrored Bufford's stance to overhear what was being said.

"Looks like a small village," Buffs told them over his shoulder, feeling confident enough to turn his head as he spoke, "we either bypass it or we rest up," he offered them.

Johnson assessed those options, thinking that a day to sleep sounded like bliss, more so that it meant he wouldn't have to take his turn carrying the unconscious woman, who, despite her slim body, still weighed too much to carry easily, because of her dead weight. Had she been able to put an arm around his neck and sit up, he would probably have been able to carry her for miles, but the pressure of keeping her head from dangling backwards dangerously made it infinitely harder to manage.

It wasn't as though handing her over to Enfield or Bufford made it any easier, as he then had to raise the unfamiliar gun and take his place at the head of the slow-moving column of people,

which qualified to the now-indigenous population as a walking buffet. Twice the woman, Astrid Larsen as she had introduced herself, had offered to help the injured Hampton and twice he good-naturedly requested that she kindly left him to it.

"Keep your hands off me and on that bloody weapon, Missy," he growled at her the last time she asked, "because if you're half as good with it as I suspect you are, then we don't want you cuddling me when it's game time."

"Resting up for the day means moving at night," Johnson answered, "which I shan't imagine is a problem for you three," he said as he used his head to indicate Larsen, Enfield and Bufford, "but he's in no fit state to creep about," he jutted his chin at Hampton, who just glowered at him, "and neither am I if I'm carrying Miss Perkins."

Travelling silently in the dark was the preferred method for Bufford, but he was accustomed to operating in teams of four, with all of them trained to the same level. Enfield, who already had the demeanour of a wraith with a resting heartrate of two beats per minute, was similarly capable, as would Hampton have been if he'd had the full use of two legs, but Johnson had to admit that he himself was far from the specialist infantry-man. He had become a manager, and civilian life held no equivalent to his position, unless it was a powerful foreman in a large plant with lots of staff who would shirk off from their duties if given any opportunity. He had become something resembling a bureaucrat, even if he could still hold his own in a fight. The biggest problem was that his way of waging war allowed him all the time in the world to deal with a slow-moving army of unthinking infantry, as he would be behind metal of differing thickness, ranging from light reconnaissance vehicles to main battle tanks, he would have numerous other similar vehicles at his disposal and would be able to combine them to bring a devastating firepower to bear on the enemy.

The only problem with that kind of warfare was that to keep his dozen or so fighting vehicles in the game, he would need a support network of at least three times that number keeping them supplied and running, and there simply weren't enough of them left.

He found himself feeling, as painful as it was to admit, a little surplus to requirements.

Astrid Larsen, with her undeniable Nordic features and stereotypically white-blonde hair, also stumped him. She was tight-lipped about her unit, revealing only that she was FSK, which as far as he knew didn't exist. However, when Bufford had muttered in his ear that she had now lost her entire team inside of a day, he stopped asking. On one of their short breaks he had asked the SBS man, in his opinion the most likely man to know, who and what she was.

"Norwegian commandos, trained to the same level as us and the Hereford boys, seeing as they are mostly free-fallers," he explained quietly, "Infiltration, erosion of infrastructure, collapsing transport and communication networks, that sort of thing. The plan was that if *Ivan* went for it, then the Norwegians would be in under cover of darkness and shut most of their western capabilities down inside of a few days. That's why people don't know about them."

"Chances are," said their quiet sniper to change the subject, "that we've missed them already." Faces turned to regard him, as often people did when he spoke, because he had the uncanny knack of appearing invisible in company.

"Possible," Hampton said, "but I think they'd either wait for us or at least send out the other helicopter to look for us."

"Unlikely," Johnson said in a solemn tone, "If it was me at the camp waiting for the final evac, I'd assume that they hadn't made it off the island, so what would be the point in wasting fuel and

risking a resource to check a negative?"

That silenced the others.

"Probably right," Bufford agreed, "under normal circumstances with full support we'd never just give up on anyone, but now? With no support and too many priorities all at once? I think they'd just look to consolidate."

"So, we find somewhere to hold up here then? Rest?" Hampton asked, unable to keep the hope out of his voice.

Heads turned to look at one another, faces showing agreement as they all submitted to the idea of sleep soon to be found. As one, with the exception of the unconscious Kimberley, all of them emitted a yelp of fright and alarm as something landed inside their discussion. The mess of dirty-looking fur emitted a chirping, meowing sound and looked up expectantly, only to flatten its ears and shoot away close to the ground, eyes wide in fright at their response.

"Fuck was that?" Hampton exclaimed in a voice far higher pitched than the others had heard come from him before, having only responded to the reactions of everyone else, as his eyes had been momentarily closed.

"Bloody cat!" Johnson said, looking around for any sign of

the creature which had disappeared as suddenly as it had emerged. All around him chuckles sounded amid gasps of breath being caught.

"Let's find somewhere before we get ambushed again," he told them, dragging himself to his exhausted feet and feeling every part of his body ache savagely, "and before I completely seize up," he added.

"Bill? You stay here with her? Enfield too," he said and received nods from them, "Shall we?" he added to the others, seeing them rise up wordlessly. Bufford nodded them forward, intending to cross the brook and approach the secluded rear of a large house.

———

"Amber!" Peter hissed desperately, as his face showed a terrible fake smile, "get your shoes on, we need to go. Now." She looked at him with wide eyes, panic evident but good sense and obedience taking over in a second. She ran, flying up the stairs and grabbing her precious things before coming back down with the lidless pot of toy soldiers and her threadbare lamb. Peter stuffed his own feet into his shoes, the oversized socks bunching uncomfortably at his toes, and grabbed the handle of the trolley by the front door.

This, he realised, had been his best idea yet. If they had to leave in a hurry, which it turned out that they now did, then he didn't want them to have to worry about supplies or going on the run with just what they could carry, so he'd loaded a small amount of food and water, which would sustain them for at least a few days. Grabbing up his pitchfork from where it rested by the front door, he dragged out the trolley and beckoned her to come with him, before reaching back and closing the door gently, so as not to announce their presence by slamming it. In an empty village, devoid of all signs of life and without any background traffic noise, a slamming door would sound like a shotgun.

As that thought hit him, so too did the handle of the shotgun as he shoved his backpack further up on his shoulders. He ignored the heavy clunk on the back of his skull, and instead surveyed the three nearest buildings that he could get to quickly.

Two of those he had cleared, but one still contained the body of the big monster who had so very nearly taken Amber, and the other was the church. His only knowledge of church was that the one his school made them go to was cold and draughty, and he reckoned very unlikely to hold food, water or beds, so he steered them straight to the house that he knew held no zombies, no bodies, but also no food or supplies, other than what they carried.

Decision made, he turned back to Amber and smiled falsely, whispering for her to follow him.

————

"Someone definitely used this as a base," Johnson said, lowering the weapon after every room had been thoroughly checked, "couple of unmade beds upstairs, all the curtains closed tight, stacked supplies..."

"So where are they?" Bufford asked. Johnson looked at him and shrugged as though that question was irrelevant right then, looking down at his boot which had caught something small and green on the floor at the foot of the stairs. Bending down to retrieve it, he held the little plastic soldier up before his eyes, twirling it slowly to take in the posing figure as it drew back one hand ready to lob a German stick grenade high in the air. Giving a small chuckle of amusement, he slipped it into a pouch without knowing why.

They went back and retrieved the others, getting wet in the

process of crossing the brook and passing Kimberley over, hand to hand, once more.

Why didn't we try to fashion a stretcher? Johnson asked himself, blaming the lack of logic on having just barely survived a helicopter crash which had killed over two thirds of the occupants. As far as excuses went, he decided that was a pretty good one.

They laid the unconscious woman on the large corner sofa and all gulped down bottles of water from the plastic-wrapped pallets. Tins were opened, and food consumed, driven by the desperate need to refuel exhausted bodies, and then they began to relax ever so slightly.

When they found themselves inside a clean environment they noticed something unpleasant. After two or three days spent constantly on the move in high-stress situations, every one of them smelt terrible, with the exception of Kimberley, who had only really joined the fight properly the night before.

Astrid made the first move, turning on the kitchen tap and watching the water fall into the wide, square sink. She let it run for a while, making a curious noise of mixed shock and pleasure.

"We have hot water," she said in awe, turning to look at the others with a smile.

"Two at a time," Johnson said, taking charge as was his natural way, "wash equipment, bodies, clothes. In that order," he added unnecessarily, knowing that the two special forces personnel and the two royal marines were unlikely to prioritise anything over their weapons and equipment.

"Looks like it'll be a hot day," Bufford added, "and that back yard isn't overlooked, so we can probably dry stuff on the patio soon."

And that was what they did, taking it in turns to step into the shower upstairs and rinse off all of their equipment, letting the water run red to brown to pale pink as they stripped down and squeezed out the garments one at a time. It took all day for the five of them to get clean and dry off, putting back on their stiff clothing to dry it the rest of the way as they sat in the sunlight streaming in through the wide kitchen windows, and they cleaned their weapons.

They ate, answered the corresponding calls of nature and found the bucket system in the downstairs toilet, which they ignored for the time being, and sometime in the afternoon, Kimberley groaned, opened one eye, and let out a cry of panic.

NINETEEN

Second Lieutenant Palmer climbed into the cab of the truck at the head of the convoy behind the only two remaining tracked vehicles. He knew his brother was there, running the whole operation and leading the shattered remnants of everyone to a new place. The helicopter took off, its belly stocked with a mixture of people and supplies, as the naval aircrew had suggested not putting all of their eggs in one basket, so to speak. As it thundered off, destined to reach their new position far more quickly than the land convoy, Palmer glanced off to his right, where the collection of a dozen men were gearing up, ready to raid the rest of the massive base, under sergeant Sinclair's leadership.

He had asked to lead the raid himself, pleading with his older brother for permission to take command, but he had resolutely denied him.

"Sergeant Sinclair's command will be wholly sufficient, I'm sure," he said coolly.

Now, devoid of all responsibility and only given a privileged seating position in the truck due to the vague respect the men had for his officer status, he nestled his gun in his lap and waited to be awarded a scrap of gainful employment. The hope, from what he had gathered from the end of the briefing he had heard but wasn't invited to, was that those dozen men would secure more fighting vehicles and ammunition to secure their new site, which he had heard was a country estate. Having experienced his fair share of such grand residences, even having grown up in one, Palmer knew what he was expecting, and that was old brick wall perimeters, ornate gates set inside them and a magnificent house in the centre. He imagined outbuildings, servants' quarters and maybe stables. Large, enclosed gardens and acres of land which would have been tended over generations, and likely a decent swathe of woodland to boot. The men, he imagined, and for that matter probably all of the civilians, would not have experienced such accommodation before and he anticipated that they would be embarrassingly impressed with the place. His disdain for the commoners returned with sudden and renewed acidity, because he had had a taste of leading men in combat and was now once again forced back into the wings to wait and try not to get killed.

He sat back and ignored his driver's attempts to engage him in conversation, like the sullen child they all imagined him to be.

———

"Keep it simple, boys," Rod Sinclair said as he checked the action of his weapon for the twentieth time and betrayed his nerves, "in and out, nothing heroic, we just grab enough and get gone."

Men shuffled their feet nervously, nodded their cautious agreement and generally worried over what was to come. Much discussion was had about the other side of the base, the place they had spent the first days of the shit-storm that had enveloped their world. The difference now, however, was that the word had spread about the so-called *Doomsday* protocol. The nuclear strikes on Europe and the Soviet Union would have untold consequences, and every man who thought about that ran his mind through the thick mud of stressful what-ifs. The consensus that they had been effectively cut off as a nation, that they had been quarantined and abandoned, led to many having dark thoughts, and without the leadership of men they believed in, they felt growing pains of hopelessness.

They set off in a loose line as they kept their footfalls soft and their eyes alert, moving through each enclosed section of the base as though it were cellular and they molecules passing through the barriers. Their progress was halting, as some sections were locked, and it forced them to take an indirect route. The helicopter crew on their flight out had passed over the area they were heading for, and had reported no signs of life, which was a bizarrely ambiguous use of words, but they did report that a section of perimeter fence appeared to be down, which was what had them all on edge. No doubt about it, they were going into contact and they had to be on their toes.

At the rear of their formation, not immediately at the back where he would be instrumental should there be any rear-guard fighting required, and far enough back from the front that any contact there would be unlikely to affect him, lurked the only man in the patrol not there voluntarily. Trooper Nevin wore a face like thunder and muttered curses to himself constantly about Sinclair, about the Captain who had been forced to intervene with a threat of shooting him for dereliction of duty, and about Johnson who had accused him of stealing supplies. Sinclair, he decided, would get them all killed. He thought he was a timid man and probably not cut out for leadership, and Nevin couldn't understand why the men followed him so eagerly. He couldn't see past his own sullen self-centred nature to fully comprehend that the men followed Sinclair because he was humble, honest and hard working. He earned men's trust instead of demanding it, which is why he did not struggle for eleven volunteers to join him. Nevin also failed to grasp why that bull of a man, Johnson, had thought it was so bad that he was using his initiative and searching the crates for anything useful. To accuse him of stealing, no matter how accurate the charge, just added to Nevin's hatred of the man who had humiliated him back on the island with a single, short punch, which, if he still thought about it, hurt him even now. He never understood why the corporals and the sergeants hated him so much, even when the officers tended to leave him alone, probably out of fear.

Not that bloody captain, though, he sneered to himself in thought, *he's a right bloody Rupert with his silver spoon up his arse. His little brother is a weasel, sure enough, but this one thinks he's a soldier.*

In truth, the reason the NCOs despised Nevin was mainly because the man was capable, very capable in fact, but at his very core he was lazy. That laziness took more concerted effort than simply performing the tasks he was given most of the time, but in their previous lives as reservists, he had never usually been under such scrutiny for so long. The only exception to this was when the squadron conducted a tour of Northern Ireland, and Nevin was focused to the point where some even considered him for promotion. Of course, as soon as they were out of real danger his attitude returned to that of the same shirking, malevolent bastard they had seen before, and any hopes of promotion were dashed. He still resented that, thinking himself better than most, but what nagged at him now was that the only time he had been expected to perform, he had panicked and a man had died.

Nevin rationalised this again, telling himself that the

death of Trooper Harris was the man's own fault for not keeping watch and not taking the warning he had given him seriously.

Wasn't my fault, Nevin had reassured himself, *stupid bastard should've listened.*

Of course, that bravado he had now convinced himself to show in his own head wasn't present when that bastard Johnson had ripped him a new one, again, and promised him punishment for it. That, he reckoned, was why he had to go on every mission there was, so that people like Johnson could force more work on his shoulders.

Well, not any more, Nevin promised himself, *first opportunity I get, I'm fucking out of here.*

And he meant it. He would look for greener grass. He would find somewhere that appreciated him. He would find another group of survivors, which he reasoned there absolutely had to be all over the place, and he would get away from the army and its bloody rules. He would live like a king, he told himself, and all he had to do was get away. His hand went inside his smock, closing around the grip of the ungainly revolver he had found, prior to being half choked by the SSM. He had all six chambers filled with the little thirty-eight bullets and another dozen loose in his trouser pocket. Despite holding his Sterling and four spare magazines for the sub machine gun, having the unexpected second world war-issued pistol made him feel safer, more prepared somehow for the mischief he intended.

Trooper Nevin, as much as he would never understand it himself, had seen death and it had made him quite insane.

"Over there," Sinclair said in a loud whisper before holding out his flat hand to the rest of them and miming a chopping motion in the rough centre of their number, effectively halving them. He wiggled the hand backwards and forwards as though he were actually trying to physically separate them and when the two men at the divide had shuffled sufficiently apart, he gave his orders.

"You men," he said to the rear group, which included Nevin, "go straight for the hangar doors and wind them open. You men," he said switching his gaze to the front of the group, "take up defensive positions at and around the entrance. You and you," he said, picking two troopers seemingly at random, "watch the flanks of the hangar. We get the easiest available vehicles, fuel them up and drive out to the armoury. I need at least one Bedford, too," he added for the tenth time as he recited their objectives, "for the small arms ammunition stores. Let's go, then."

The men nodded back at his anxious face, and he led them out.

————

Almost a month before Sinclair's small detachment tiptoed their way back into the base from the far side of its multitude of fences and walls, and shortly after they had first fled in the night, the large building they had used to house the civilians in a hurry, had been one of the last places to be evacuated. In that haste to get out, the building had not been checked, not that a sweep of that building would probably have prevented the sequence of events that had followed. One woman, in an attempt to sleep in relative peace, was tucked away in a small cupboard with a green army sleeping bag when the call to evacuate had so unexpectedly come.

As much as the army loved lists, the woman had been missed off their rota when they had ended up on the island, as there were simply too many things to do and too few people to organise them.

They had abandoned the base just in time, closing up the gates behind them in an attempt to keep it clear of infestation for as long as possible, but they had no way of knowing back then that they had only narrowly avoided total annihilation at the hands, *teeth* even, of a small swarm of them approaching through the shrouded woodland behind them. That swarm, driven on by the cacophony of engines and gunfire, converged on one section of perimeter fence and the combined weight of their moaning, hissing, clawing bodies collapsed it to pour them through the gap like so much water through a drain. The swarm dissipated once inside, spreading out to advance in a seemingly unending mass, all heading in the general direction of the main gate where the last stimulating noises had come from. It was as though the zombies shuffled along with some half-blind and half-remembered sense of purpose until something warm blooded presented itself.

The woman slept on, her ears stuffed with twists of toilet paper to block out the noises of so many people crammed into one place, so she had no idea that the ground outside the building was now crawling with the people the soldiers were calling Screechers.

A woman in a skirt and blouse, streaked with dried blood and filth and her high-shouldered matching jacket torn half off her, walked oddly with stiff legs as she rose and fell a few inches every time she put down her right foot. So advanced was her skill and experience at wearing the high heels, that she had miraculously retained one of them. The other foot, bare below the torn remains of her tights, scraped on the tarmac as she veered away to the building which still smelled faintly of something that her subconscious brain told her was edible. Her hair was a mess, but her face seemed strangely unblemished, with the exception of one long, thin scrape caused by a low branch of a tree as she had advanced through the woodland, not knowing why. That mostly flawless face, with its two milky-white eyes set above the scratch, locked onto the doors of the building and her body followed. Pushing into the doors and bouncing back slightly, her hands raised in another half-remembered gesture and her body went forwards again, applying enough pressure through her outstretched palms to force the aperture open. On hearing the bumps and creak of doors, two other zombies split away from the edges of the crowd and headed towards the new sounds without knowing why. They followed the woman on one high heel through the door and into a large room where the smell of living people filled their nostrils and sparked them into more animated action. They stomped through the room in ungainly, uncoordinated actions, knocking things over as they went.

Waking cramped up and in need of a thorough stretch, the woman pulled the twists of paper from her ears and worked her jaw to rid herself of the stiffness. As she did, she froze in the dark, hearing a muffled noise from outside. A noise wasn't anything to worry about in itself, and she couldn't place her finger on *why* the noise disturbed her, but her spine tingled, and her breathing doubled in speed to become shallow as her body flushed with adrenaline.

Inching the door open outwards into the corridor, her eye caught movement off to the right. As soon as she saw the woman with one high heel, she pulled back and shut the door, banging it just loud enough to know that she had been heard. Holding her breath and gripping the door handle with all her strength, the tears began to flow down her face as she heard the faint, 'click, slap,' of uneven footsteps coming for her. The sound stopped at its loudest, and the sudden noise of the zombie's face banging into the door elicited a scream of such volume that it was answered threefold.

The woman screamed, drawing in breath just as the response came from the other side of the thin wood. The racking, shrieking intake of breath through a ravaged throat promised the woman such a malicious death that she cried again, sobbing as she gripped onto the door handle with all her might. Two other shrieks responded in addition to the first, signalling the anticipated feeding frenzy to come when they unearthed their trapped quarry.

Those shrieks carried outside through the doors and to the ears of other zombies. Every one of them to hear it turned and made for the doors to push their way inside and cram into the back corridor, where the shrieks were incessant outside a cupboard door. Those who didn't hear the initial screams followed the ones closer to the building who had detected it, and they were sparked by the movement to follow and cram inside until the building could hold no more bodies.

Those who had either bypassed or been ahead of the noisy discovery simply wandered away, stimulated by an elusive bit of wildlife or by far-off noises, but those inside the building had been trapped inside by the need to pull a door to leave. They could easily have crushed their way through the doors, but the outside world offered no reason to get riled up and spark such action. Inside the besieged cupboard, the woman screamed and sobbed her way into hyperventilation and eventually unconsciousness, until the combined weight of bodies outside which could not grasp and turn the round door knob broke through the plasterboard wall instead. The renewed screams from inside were short-lived as the woman was grabbed by dirty hands and ragged nails and pulled through the gaps to be ripped apart and devoured in the narrow corridor.

Like some grim and grotesque approximation of crowd-surfing at a rock concert, the woman's body never landed on the ground, not in any entirety at least, as she was pulled open and eaten above head height by the fifty or so pairs of hands that reached for her. She never returned, never came back as one of them, because there was nothing left of her to reanimate within seconds of being discovered. Although she suffered an unimaginable, horrendous death, at least for the woman who had tried to find some peace in quiet sleep, her nightmare was over.

———

There were over three hundred zombies crammed shoulder to shoulder in that building for over a month. Nothing outside had managed to stir them into action and they seemed to slow down and stand still in some form of hibernation. They simply stood, swaying in silence, waiting for something to spark them into undead life once more. That stimulus, that spark to ignite their hunger once again, came in the form of thirteen soldiers pausing just outside the back corner of the building for orders to be hissed.

"Let's go then," Sinclair hissed, totally unaware that he had just awoken the beast.

TWENTY

The country residence teemed with life as if it were an ant colony, only instead of the ants there were military personnel and civilians mucking in together to make the grounds as impenetrable to the undead as possible. Despite the obvious military leadership, the nearly one hundred people milling about were almost half civilian and seemed to be operating under the army control quite happily. Not all of them were able, obviously, and one large reception room which Captain Palmer stated with confidence was the drawing room, had become a haven for the young and the old or incapacitated together.

Not the incapacitated soldiers, however, for even the injured men could be propped up to keep watch.

That contingent appeared to fall under the leadership of Denise Maxwell who, after being reunited with her husband, had taken to her own new and unofficial role of senior NCO with as much practicality and necessary enthusiasm as her husband had, despite the terrible circumstances leading to his elevation.

Cooper, the tall man from Admin Troop who was usually

flanking the now missing and presumed dead Sergeant Croft, had been one of the only members of his sub unit to survive, and as such was now following the captain with a clipboard liberated from the kitchens. Three surviving officers, not counting the Special Air Service's Major Downes, who was off doing who knew what, paced the ground floor with a small entourage. There was a fourth officer to have survived, but the Colonel had been in need of a lie down when he arrived at the house, so he was shown to one of the larger bedroom suites, and most likely slept through all of the hustle and bustle taking place on a floor below him.

"Mister Maxwell?" Palmer senior said, slightly louder than his conversational tone, as though stopping and turning to find the man would break the flow of productivity.

"Sir?"

"Organise a small detachment, mechanically-minded people if we have enough, and send them to the nearest farms. I want heavy machinery, diggers specifically and two of them ideally. Also, we need sufficient fuel for them, and a report on anything else useful, such as building materials and the like."

"Ooh, ooh, hold on a second, Sir?" Cooper said as he almost dropped his clipboard, attempting to find a note on a sheet clipped towards the back.

"Aha!" he declared, finding the piece of paper he wanted and unclipping it whilst simultaneously managing to drop half of the other papers and the clipboard, to be left holding a scrap of paper and half a pencil stub. The whole procession stopped to regard him and made his embarrassment far worse, so he spoke with a quiet voice and flushed cheeks.

"The farm on this estate, Sir," he said, "there's a digger on there. It's on the report from the *Sass* blokes."

"Sergeant?" Palmer said as he turned towards Maxwell.

"I'll sort two teams," he replied, "one for here and one for other farms. I'll ask the Major if he doesn't mind doing one of them."

"Good man," Palmer said as he turned and resumed the procession, leaving Trooper Cooper to scurry and catch up after snatching the loose paper from the old, thick carpet.

"Now," Palmer said, changing the subject as he glanced at his watch, "when are we expecting Sergeant Sinclair and his men?"

———

From the air, a view which only a very few of them had enjoyed, the estate they had selected looked ideal for their needs in enough ways to make them choose it as soon as it was found. Judging by the ornate building's front and high brick wall extending around most of the grounds, the Palmer brothers employed their classical education and declared the estate to be very early Victorian, most likely planned and built almost one hundred years before. A trooper had found a plaque near the large front doors which indeed proved the officers right, detailing the years it had been commissioned and completed as 1891 and 1895 respectively.

The main house had a four-storey central square and a three-storey wing either side of that with a curious rectangular lump added on to one wing, which had housed a larger and more modern kitchen built in the fifties. There were numerous outbuildings forming part of the ready-made defences, including stables which had been converted into garaging, as well as a massive coal bunker and log store. All of these buildings had been painstakingly checked and cleared, and the entire place declared empty. Various opinions had been offered about why, but in Palmer's view, the rich occupants were likely to have been skiing at that time of year in the Alps, or enjoying some time in their European residence, which would fashionably be on the southern coast of France near to Nice.

There were food stores, not enough to sustain them all through the next winter, obviously, but there were still untouched harvests of ripening maize to reap in nearby fields. The boxed supplies they had brought with them would sustain their people for months, but on calorific value alone and not volume.

They had to supplement, and they had to think fast about it.

The day wore on, passing the midday point and those not actively engaged in strenuous tasks began to worry about the failure of the others to arrive. People consoled themselves and offered their own silent hopes that the men were loading up as much hardware as they could find to bring back to their warm new home in the sun. Not many had the opportunity to sit and worry, as tasks were dished out to small groups of men and women alike, and those tasks ranged from creating an inventory of the food stores in the vast cellar under the kitchen, to estimating the amount of solid fuel remaining for the fires. Most people hadn't realised yet, but without significant stores of wood and coal and oil for the heating, the coming winter was looking to become a fight for survival against more than just zombies.

The two patrols went out, the SAS men returning first with a digger to hand over their prize and report to a team of three men from One Troop, who began to use the narrower rear bucket on the machine to excavate a trench, under the orders of captain Palmer.

"Fifty yards out," he ordered simply, "working west from the driveway. Six feet deep and six feet wide." He received only nods of compliance and verbal affirmations of his instructions.

They went to work, creating the barrier which would slow the advance of any concentrated attack for time enough to emplace heavy guns, and also to prevent the straying of zombies in ones and twos into their safe area. There were men on patrol around the perimeter and others on standby in two Fox cars, which contained almost all of the ammunition left for the vehicles, ready to react to any concentration of enemy and cut them down. That ammunition, those 30mm rounds for the small cannons and the linked bullets for the machine guns, were a finite resource. Just as the bullets for their personal weapons were.

The only thing that wouldn't run out of ammunition would be their bayonets, but for trained soldiers to be forced to rely on cold steel, that would sap morale faster than ice sapped body heat.

The only thing to be done was to stay busy, prepare their defences, and hope.

By mid-afternoon, Palmer had gone to find the crew of their only remaining helicopter. Lieutenant Commander Barrett and his co-pilot Lieutenant James Morris were playing cards in silence at a table made of dark wood and spindly and elaborately carved legs in one of the grand bedrooms they had adopted as their quarters, while their loadmaster snored gently on the chaise longue underneath the high window.

"Gentlemen," Palmer said as he knocked twice on the open door, passing through it, "I was wondering if I might..." he trailed away, his nose involuntarily twitching at some newly-detected smell that broke through his normally impeccable manners to contort his face.

"I say," he asked quietly, "what in God's name is that odour?"

"That, Captain," Morris said with evident amusement, "would be the boots of Chief Petty Officer Brinklow. You're trained for biological attacks, I presume? What course of action would you suggest?"

"I'd suggest burning the man's boots for starters," Palmer

responded before he could gather himself, "and possibly some-thing similar for the man himself."

Both pilots chuckled their amusement at his disgust and retort.

"Captain," Barrett said, as he regarded his hand before selecting one card to lay down and make Morris huff a sound of annoyance, "believe me when I say you get used to it after a short time. I honestly can't even detect it any longer."

"I'll have to take your word for that, I'm afraid," Palmer said, getting back to business, "I wonder if I could impose on your time?"

Both pilots laid down their cards and paid him their full attention to betray their professionalism. They may have appeared to have been doing nothing, but their reaction showed just how ready they were to be needed.

"I have some concerns," Palmer began, "concerns I obvi-ously don't wish to share among the men and the civilians, you understand, and I would like you to conduct a reconnaissance for me."

"The other helicopter?" Morris asked.

"Yes, primarily," Palmer said, "and also, I'd have rather expected that the men left to gather more arms at the base would have been back by now, or at least made contact. I've just checked with Corporal Daniels, who is rather uncomfort-ably posted inside the Sultan in this heat, and he hasn't heard from anyone."

"Absolutely," Barrett said, seeing Palmer deflate ever so slightly with relief, "However we don't have sufficient fuel to do that. We'd need to refuel somewhere before any of that, and the only fuel reserves we know of are in areas that we also know to be overrun. You see the predicament?"

Palmer clearly did see the predicament. His right hand reached up and scratched the four days of stubble on his chin and cheeks, giving him the look of a much rougher man than he was. His thoughtful pause paid off, as Brinklow spoke from the gaudy one-sided couch in the room. His snoring had faded away without any of the officers noticing and he had come awake silently to listen to the conversation.

"The island is out, obviously," he said as he swung his legs down and slipped them into his boots. Palmer felt as though the source of the smell had been plugged, or at least muted in some way when he did this, "and as far as I know, there's none left at the base. The only other option I can think of is going back to Yeovilton."

His suggestion silenced the room as the others waited for the logic behind the idea to explain itself. When nobody spoke, Brinklow gave the explanation himself.

"We know we can reach it with what we've got left, and we know there was a lot of fuel there when we left. It's unlikely that it's all gone because unless someone went back with a few tankers and emptied it in the last month, then it's still there. The only downside is that we don't know how many of the Bitey Bastards are there now. Sirs," he added weakly to defend his gruff language.

Palmer turned to the pilots, who in turn looked at each other, then shrugged and looked back at the army captain.

"Makes sense," Morris said.

"We'd need some boys to defend us as we refuelled, obviously," Barrett added.

"I'll ask Lieutenant Lloyd," Palmer said, "his men should at least be more familiar with the base than my chaps."

"And they are the specialist infantry," Morris added, wincing immediately as he had spoken without thinking, "obviously your men have fought bravel…"

"I understood your point, Lieutenant," Palmer interrupted to save time spent having his ego massaged, "I'll see to it. What time frame?"

"As soon as possible," Barrett said, rising from his chair,

"we'll start pre-flight checks now. We'll start the search at the island and work out from there, assuming we have fuel."

Palmer nodded to them and left, remembering as soon as he had moved from the room that the marines officer was deployed and their sergeant currently missing. Grabbing a soldier from his former headquarters troop to first check his current duty and finding it less important than the task he wanted, he sent the man to find any of the marines and ask who their most senior man was on site.

"I shall be downstairs," he told the man, "tell them to find me there." As he spoke, another thought struck him, "And after that, find the SAS Major and request that he speak to me."

The man had done his job quickly, resulting in the tall and seemingly bored Royal Marine medic arriving and offering a tired salute to the captain.

"Corporal Sealey, Sir," he said in a thickly accented voice that made him sound almost bored.

"And you are the senior man?" Palmer asked.

"I think so, Sir, with Mister Lloyd out and about with the other corporal and Sergeant Hampton... not here... then I guess I'm it."

Palmer nodded and was saved from saying anything further on the matter as the tall man wearing black walked in and nodded to them both. Marine corporal and army captain returned the nod and Downes turned to face Palmer expectantly, with his eyebrows raised.

"I'll get right to it, then," he said to the two summoned men in the small parlour they occupied, "I want to send out the helicopter with the purpose of finding the other aircraft and giving us some definitive answers about what happened. I also wish to chase up the detachment still at the base. The crew are preparing to leave soon; however, I need a security detail for them as they will need to return to their original station for refuelling. The status of that base is unknown. My thoughts were to send our marines, since they would have knowledge of the base, but I rather fear they have somewhat depleted numbers, given that they are currently out on mission. Corporal Sealey here is the senior man currently."

"That said, Sir," Sealey said, "I'm the team medic," he explained, pointing out that, whilst a trained and experienced commando, he was not a usual leader of men in action.

"I'll take my team, if you wish?" Downes said, knowing that the offer was expected and hoped for. "Saves my chaps getting stagnant," he added almost jovially. He had stripped off his smock to reveal thick arms with the sleeves of his black top pulled up and bunched above his elbows. Given the size of his forearms, the chance of them slipping back down unintentionally was almost negligible.

Palmer thanked them both, let Sealey off the hook to return to his duties preparing the house and grounds for defence, and indicated for Downes to stay a while. He walked to the window, looking out over a palatial inner courtyard with enough tended grass to grow crops for half of them, and he let out a sigh of near mental exhaustion.

"You're doing a fine job, Julian," Downes told him gently, "making the best of what we have here."

"Thank you, Major," he said.

"Clive," he said, making Palmer realise that he had never actually given the unnervingly quiet Major his first name.

"What were you before?" Palmer asked, "Before your current post, if you don't mind my asking?"

"Not at all," Downes said, "I was the cliché as it happens. Paras, served my first stint with the Regiment as a troop boss," he said, meaning his own regiment, as all soldiers said of their military family, "and was invited back as a Major. Only one of mine is a Para, the other two are what everyone calls Crap-Hats. I doubt it matters now, but we were in Afghanistan for the last nine months nearly, playing Cold War games with the whole *enemy of my enemy* thing."

The way he spoke showed that his education was at least mostly equal to Palmer's, perhaps not as expensive as the boarding schools he and his brother had attended but definitely privately funded. He had lost the upper-class edge of that education and accent now, probably because of the company he had kept and by not being insulated from his men, as officers in regular army units would naturally be. He had lived and breathed as one of the men, had forgone any sense of entitlement for himself or servitude from his men, and that bond seemed far stronger than the discipline of Palmer's own rag-tag squadron.

"I'd heard of such clandestine missions," Palmer said, "all very *secret squirrel*," he said with a smirk as he used the terminology of his men.

"Very," Downes said, "but I honestly felt for our Russian enemies in that hell hole. To be conscripted and barely trained, then sent into the most inhospitable place on God's green earth, barring the Borneo jungle in the wet season maybe, where your enemy sneaks around in the dark to cut your *comrades*," he said this in a Slavic accent and rolled his R's theatrically, "to pieces so you can hear their screams all night is just barbaric."

He trailed off, leaving them both in thoughtful silence before Downes slapped the younger man lightly on the back.

"Give me a straight-up zombie fight any day," he said nonchalantly. "We'll talk when I'm back, Captain. Keep up the good work."

TWENTY-ONE

They gorged themselves, relatively speaking, on the stores of canned food stacked neatly in the house. Without bothering to heat anything, a hardship that didn't seem the slightest bit important to people who had operated in or trained for war, they took it in turns to spin the handle of the opener and tuck greedily into the contents.

Johnson peeled back the metal lids of two tins, shoved a fork and a spoon into them without recalling what went in which tin, and walked over to where Kimberley was propped up in the middle of multiple cushions, with her right leg elevated on yet more soft cushions.

"Thank you, Dean," she said with a hint of an awkward smile. He held out the can to her, furrowed his brow and switched hands to offer her the other.

"Fruit salad," he said, "I've got baked beans if you wanted those instead…"

"No, no," she said weakly, "fruit salad is fine."

"You need the sugar," Johnson said as he sat beside her as lightly as possible, yet still crushing the settee under his bulk. "Make sure you drink all the syrup; build up your strength."

"She needs fluids and rest," came the unintentionally harsh-sounding voice of Astrid Larsen, "but I suppose that this *fruits salad* will be good." Johnson nodded, rising to leave Kimberley in the capable hands of the medic, whilst he stalked away to find a place to sit and eat his cold beans. Dropping himself down on another settee next to the injured Bill Hampton, Johnson froze with his shoulders hunched until the foul stream of hissed swear words finished pouring from the marine's mouth. Glancing across at him, he saw the man fixing him with an evil gaze which no doubt would have terrified the young marines under his command.

Johnson, however, was no twenty-something marine, and returned the look with his own thousand-yard stare. His look didn't silence a platoon or two of marines, it cut through an entire squadron's chatter as well as the sounds of their engines, to focus over a hundred minds on his next words. The two men stayed like that for a second, trapped in some approximation of stags locking horns until one backed away to avoid injury.

"Watch me fucking leg," Hampton muttered as he looked back down at his own tin of cold food.

"Sorry, Bill," Johnson said as he leaned back and stirred the contents of his own tin to realise that he had given himself the fork and Kimberley the spoon for her fruit salad.

Fuck it, he thought, licking the fork clean and tipping the tin up to his mouth to drink the contents like an especially thick, cold soup. Hampton was wearing boxer shorts, fresh socks from his own kit and a T-shirt which was fractionally too small for him. Still a very fit and strong man, he had run ever so slightly to fat, having spent more time sitting at a desk due to his rank and responsibilities, and the shirt showed up the bits he might not want people seeing. Johnson looked at him and decided that he probably couldn't care less what anyone thought of him. His swollen right knee was propped up and looked angry where the bruising was already starting to show.

Larsen sat with Kimberley, checking that she was still making sense after the bang to her head sustained in the crash had left her unconscious for almost a day. When she had come around, screaming terribly as her last memory was that of being in a helicopter dropping unexpectedly from the sky, Astrid had calmed her, filled her in on what had happened, and taken her away to the bathroom where she cut away her clothes and washed her, tending to each injury as she discovered it. They hadn't noticed throughout the remainder of the night or the first part of the day as they carried her because she was wearing black denim jeans, but she had sustained a nasty cut to the inside of her thigh which refused to stop opening up and bleeding if she moved.

Muffled cries could be heard by the men downstairs as she sat still and bit down on a towel as Astrid put three stitches in the wound before cleaning the rest of her. That injured leg was now elevated on cushions to keep the blood from pooling around the injury and putting pressure on the stitches. She was flushed pink after being scrubbed clean with the last of the hot water, and dressed in oversized jogging bottoms and a sweatshirt, both emblazoned with some American university logo and name.

As Johnson sat beside Hampton, both eating their cold meal in grumpy silence, Bufford returned to the large, open-plan living area after coming down the stairs.

"Your man is keeping watch," he said to Hampton, meaning Enfield, the marine sniper, "not that there's much to see, but he insists. I've given him another can of scran and told him to get washed up because he's honkin'. The water's icers now, but he's not bothered. He could do with his slug because he looks ready to cream in."

Hampton nodded sagely and chewed before swallowing and opening his mouth to respond to the SBS man in front of him, but then he put a finger to his lips and burped around it, before wincing and hitting himself in the chest lightly to somehow ease the heartburn and indigestion he was feeling.

"Yeah, we're all chinstraps, mate, but his oppo got zapped in the crash. Inseparable those two were. Leigh and Enfield; spotter and sniper. Couldn't fucking write it," he paused for them to chuckle, "but they were A1, mate. Gen."

It was Bufford's turn to nod sagely then, sparing a thought for the other marines who hadn't made it out, before Hampton changed the subject again.

"Mate of mine went SB in '83. Steve Priest?" Hampton asked hopefully.

"C Squadron," Bufford answered immediately with a straight face, "good guy."

"Yeah," Hampton laughed lightly, "fucker for biting though. Always easy to get a wind up on him."

Buffs smiled at his memory, saying, "I'll spell him upstairs, make sure he hits his grot soon," and walked away leaving Johnson and Hampton alone again.

Johnson finished his tin of beans, using the pointless fork to scrape the rest of the juice towards the edge where he slurped it into his mouth. Wiping his face with his hand he turned to Hampton and asked, "Is that why your training takes so damned long?"

"What you on about?" Hampton asked back, suspecting that he was being set up for an inter-military jibe.

"You have to learn a new language when you go on your long, romantic walks, camping in Devon. English is just fine for everyone, you know?"

"Fuck off, pongo," Hampton responded with a smirk.

"Seriously though, is Enfield going to be alright?"

"He'll manage," Hampton answered sincerely, "no idea what he'll be like when the job's done, but he'll manage for now."

"When the job's done?" Johnson nearly scoffed. "When's

that going to be?"

"Fuck knows," Hampton said, his tongue protruding from one side of his mouth as he spun his can spanner, which had appeared from a pouch on his kit resting beside him, and he attacked another can, this time ravioli.

The two men sat in silence just as the two women in the same large room sat in quiet conversation. Footfalls above them denoted where Bufford and Enfield traded places for one to stand guard whilst the other washed, and shortly afterwards the sniper made his way down the stairs wearing some ill-fitting shirt and loose trousers over his slim frame. He nodded to both his sergeant and the army sergeant major, and laid out a towel on the low coffee table before resting first his salvaged L85 on the cloth to strip and clean it. Then he rebuilt it and checked the action to load a magazine, ready to go to work. The big sniper rifle came next, the big bolt being drawn back, and the breech cleaned almost with a tenderness.

"You're good with that," Johnson said blandly, unsure himself if it was a question or a statement.

"I'm alright," Enfield said, "I'm just lucky that it makes sense to me when it doesn't for others. On the sniper course the staff hated me because I just understood how things worked; wind, distance, elevation, relative elevation between shooter and target, air density, humidity, rainfall, curvature of the earth; all things that people had to learn the hard way, but they just make sense to me. So yeah, I'm alright with it, but I'll only be alright with it another forty-six times, if you get my meaning."

Johnson did.

"And with the other one?" he asked, pointing at the new bullpup rifle.

"Less so," Enfield said after regarding it for a time, "but I have a hundred chances more with that than this," he said nodding between the guns as he packed up the cleaning kit and rolled it tight to fit back into his pouches.

"Speaking of that," Johnson said as he groaned and creaked his way to standing up, "Miss Larsen, could I borrow you?"

Astrid patted Kimberley's leg as she stood and walked towards the kitchen and Johnson's direction, carrying the empty food tins.

"Sergeant Major?" she asked, her accent making the enquiry sound formal.

"I was hoping you could give me a run-down on stripping this?" he asked, holding up the suppressed MP5 she had given him, "I'm assuming it needs cleaning..."

Astrid picked up her own identical weapon and sat at the white kitchen table. Johnson searched the drawers under the granite worktop and located what he wanted on the third attempt, selecting two tea towels and laying one down as a kind of placement, whilst offering the other to the hard, blonde woman. She took it silently, laying out the cloth just as he had. Johnson sat beside her, better placed to mimic her movements without his brain trying to switch the left and the right.

"Charging handle back, verify empty chamber, remove rear stock pin, remove folding stock," she said with an air of robotics as though she was literally translating the manual in her head into English, "hinge down the lower mechanism and slide back charging handle, remove bolt and carrier assembly," she went on, performing one task at a time and waiting for him to copy the actions, "rotate bolt head, locking piece, firing pin and spring all come out. There it is," she said, opening her hands to demonstrate just how simple it was. Johnson rebuilt the gun, making the same movements in reverse until it was whole again, before stripping it down a second time as Astrid watched. She only had to correct him once, and after that he had the task down and began to clean the working parts. She had stripped, cleaned and oiled her weapon before he had finished, but stayed to watch. Of the four magazines he had for the weapon, Johnson found only two of them to be fully stocked, so he stripped the bullets from the spare magazines for his Sterling, which had been lost in the crash. Discarding the old magazines as they had none of those weapons left, he stored the handful of spare rounds in a pouch, ready to refill the magazines, and returned his webbing and weapon to where they rested against the stairs along with the others.

Clean, fed and resting, the six battered survivors from the second helicopter lapsed into uncertain silence.

Amber cried. She hadn't cried since Peter had first found her, but now she buried her small face into his only slightly larger chest and sobbed quietly. He didn't know what upset her most; it could've been the fear of having to rush out so suddenly after waking or, more likely he guessed, she was upset that the cat had not come with them.

They had fled in plenty of time to avoid the people, and Peter didn't dare close the curtains overlooking their former squat now, for fear that anyone there would notice the change. As a result, they were forced to live at the back of the house and avoid the front rooms, which meant that they were limited to existing in the kitchen downstairs and the bathroom and a small bedroom upstairs. He considered leaving the village again, just packing up whatever they could carry and running out of the back, but that would take them back in the direction they had first come from and that felt too much like defeat. He would go in a different direction, but the careful glances he stole at their old house showed the figure of a man watching through the partially open curtains. Any flight out the rear of the house would no doubt be noticed, and he wanted to avoid these people at any cost.

As he sat with her, long after she had finished crying, now just pressing her head into him to emit the occasional spasm of breathing in, he flashed back to the reason he was besieged by fear.

The things, the monsters, the *ex*-people; they terrified him well enough and with good reason, but the people were somehow worse. He didn't understand why he had a hard time trusting adults, and he didn't realise the impact of the neglect and abuse he had experienced, but that mistrust and fear was solidified when he had watched Amber's mother being dragged away unconscious, leaving behind a helpless girl. He had been the helpless one once, and he'd had his older sister to protect and shield him from the harsher realities of life, but now his innocence, whatever was left of it, his naivety was gone. It had died with his mother, or his dog as he couldn't be sure which one of the two hateful creatures he was upset about, and it had died with the disappearance of his sister and father before that. It had disappeared with the sickening slaughter of the farm animals at the hands and teeth of the crowd of monsters which had swept through to wipe his home off the face of the earth.

All of these factors and experiences combined to form a hard casing around his personality, and the final part of that armour was watching men drag away a woman and leave her little girl behind.

"I'll never leave you," he whispered to her, stroking her hair and shushing her softly, "I'll never leave you."

And he wouldn't. He swore it to her and to himself. He would wait out the day and lead her towards yet more uncertain safety to avoid the terror of what the men would do to her.

Her breathing had softened, become deeper and more rhythmic, to tell him that she had fallen asleep in his arms despite
not having long woken. It was the stress, he supposed. Just as
he closed his eyes to rest with her for a time and pass the day in
safety and silence, a sound threw him straight back into the
fight for survival.

TWENTY-TWO

"Can't sit here all day," Bufford said, "perimeter is insecure. I want to push it out, who's coming?"

Johnson rose to his feet, cursing every part of his body that ached, which he realised with annoyance, was every part of his body. They had changed back into their uniforms by the afternoon, having washed and mostly dried them, and shrugged back into their equipment harnesses. Astrid Larsen stood and put on her kit, her slim frame carrying the black equipment with uncommon ease as she checked that Kimberley would be fine without her.

The woman with the scarred face waved her away, telling her not to fuss over her and that she felt like a nuisance. Those protestations were ignored as Astrid checked the dilation of her pupils once more.

"Any severe headaches or bad dizziness, send for me," she told Hampton, who was still established on the other settee with his swollen knee raised. He had allowed Enfield to clean his rifle, and he sat with it resting across his lap, facing the front door as a guard. Enfield readied himself to go with them, the huge and angular rifle strapped diagonally across his back, and the four of them made ready to move out.

Hampton watched, amused and interested in how the concept of rank had gone out of the window. None of those who had survived the crash were regular soldiers; not one of them a uniform filler by any stretch of the imagination. He was a royal marine sergeant, and the lowest ranking of them was a specialist commando sniper with skills far beyond the others in many senses. The bearded man from the special forces was evidently a former marine, as his lingo paid testimony to, and nobody achieved an NCO rank in special forces without being any good. Johnson, despite being what Hampton would unkindly call a weekend warrior or a hobby soldier, was evidently an experienced and capable man, having achieved the highest rank available without become a member of the officer class. His own officer, Lloyd, could be forgiven any scorn for being one of them, because unlike the army, the royal marines officers lived and fought as one of the team and had to pass the same tests as their men, instead of sipping sherry and brandy and relying on family connections like the other branches. The anomaly for Hampton was the Norwegian woman. She had been very quiet, probably due to the same loss that all of them felt for the dead left behind in a burning aircraft, but her loss would be worse as she was now the only one left of her team and her countrymen. She was totally alone, and to make it worse for her, even Hampton couldn't comprehend how a woman could be a frontline soldier, let alone a highly trained one. He kept his misogynistic thoughts to himself, not that he saw much wrong with the blatantly sexist ideas bouncing around his brain, as she had done nothing but prove herself capable since he had first met her.

Now, watching the four of them stack up by the front door ready to move out, he saw the natural abilities and training of those most suited to the task taking over. All of them would be

CQB and FIBUA trained; that is to say they had been taught to engage the enemy in close-quarter battle and fight in built-up areas. Indeed, he and Enfield had attended the same refresher training before their last Northern Ireland deployment. He also knew from conversation that Johnson had toured there, so he would have had the same level of training, albeit to a far lesser degree, as the man was a tankie. The SB man, Buffs, would be able to do room clearances in his sleep, and if he had to guess, the woman, Astrid, would have done a fair bit of that kind of work too.

The natural selection of leadership seemed to evolve before his eyes as the most experienced took the lead, with the second best at his shoulder. The third strongest link would be taking up the rear and the weakest of their small team would be placed third in line where he wouldn't have to make any decisions to engage without following a lead. The senior man, the highest ranking, fell into place to learn the tactics of special forces room clearing fast and, on the job, not once complaining or trying to force a plan on the others. Hampton's appreciation for the man went up then, as he liked to see humility where it counted.

"On me, alternate eyes left and right," Buffs said, "at the door we check, do a perimeter in twos, then go in. I want the nearest houses cleared one by one. We start with the church, head along that side of the road for three houses, then cross over. That gives us a buffer we know is clear at least. Questions?"

There were none. They moved out, eyes wired for any threat, and the first two people in the team feeling only slightly out of sorts for operating in a clandestine manner during bright sunshine. The church was reached within seconds, with Bufford pointing at himself and Enfield, then pointing a flat palm held vertically like a blade and indicating that they would head around the left side of the building. He pointed at Larsen and Johnson in turn, making the same hand gesture around to the right. The instructions were given fast and clean with no misunderstanding, and he hoped that he would not need to repeat them so long-windedly for the next house.

That was the problem with operating at a level of elite excellence; nothing else compared or came close when you had to work with men who didn't have the benefit of that training.

Johnson nodded at his partner, both moving off as Bufford pointed at Enfield's SA80 and wagged a finger before pointing at his own suppressed submachine gun. Enfield nodded, clicking on the bayonet to demonstrate that he would not fire a noisy shot unless absolutely necessary.

The big man and the slim but strong woman crept around the side of the church, finding a small stone bridge spanning a brook which trickled and bubbled away beneath. A rotting stench filled their nostrils, forcing both of them to react in disgust. Johnson peered over the edge to see the whitened, bloated and decaying body lying flat on its back in the shallow water, and a wide-eyed blind stare of white eyeballs bored back up at him. He peered at it, knowing it to be twice dead from the wound in its head. He found Larsen's eye and indicated that the thing had been stabbed through the skull. She nodded at the information, knowing its relevance and adding it to the evidence of survivors in the village. Or at least that there had been some recently. They continued, meeting the others at the rear of the churchyard, where Johnson indicated for Buffs and Enfield to go back around their way. He pointed out the corpse, indicating again in silence that it had been rendered safe in an effective manner which wasn't often seen before the world went to flesh-eating shit. Buffs nodded his understanding, no doubt filing the information away just as effectively as Astrid had, then he led the way back to the front where a small crowbar was produced from down his back. Jemmying the heavy wooden doors open with ease, the team poured in and checked the few rooms.

The smell of death hit them immediately. Despite the warm weather outside and the direct sunlight that was pleasantly hot, the air inside was cool and damp and laced with the musty stench of death. The source of the smell was discovered in one of the cloisters and the disturbed flies buzzed angrily away from the remnants of the vicar's hanging body. Beside the wooden pulpit which had tipped on its side, no doubt as the man's final act, lay next to it a writhing pile of gore where the maggots fed on the filth leaking from his body. Entire chunks of the man had fallen away, decayed from the inside by the gruesome act of nature and the passage of time.

They all took in the scene and all withdrew to search the building for anything of use. Some small supplies of food, mainly biscuits and the makings of hot drinks, went into a bag they found, to be deposited on the front doorstep. Bufford's pointed instructions made it clear that they would check and search every building and come back for the haul after the work was done. Shutting the door on the church, they cast their minds to the next property.

The front door was stubborn and very locked. Without firing weapons or kicking it in with enough noise to bring unwelcome attention down on them, the team went back around their perimeter to try the back door. The splintering of the wood from the heaving crowbar sounded louder than gunfire but the old wood refused to budge, instead bending and not allowing them access. A snap of Astrid's fingers sounded, and she waited until the three men looked at her before pointing upwards to a partially open first floor window. Buffs and Johnson cupped their hands and hoisted her high up to watch as she gripped the exposed window frame with one hand and pushed up the locking bar to swing the opening wide. She hauled herself the rest of the way, slipping through the veil of a net curtain to shoot an upturned thumb back out. Soft sounds came from inside the house as she made her way down the stairs. A strained click and a metallic scrape indicated that the back door was unlocked.

The door creaked open to show her in the ready stance with the parachute stock of the gun tight into her shoulder as she leaned into the weapon and pressed her face against it to aim down the barrel.

"Upstairs clear," she whispered as the others joined her inside and Enfield shut the door quietly, "but you can smell this, yes?". They could smell it. The same sickly, vile odour as before, and as they advanced on the few rooms downstairs a scene unfolded which further solidified their belief that someone capable was operating in this tiny village long after the fall of everything.

A zombie, a bloody big one even by Johnson's standards, lay face down on the living room rug with its head haloed by a small puddle of dark filth. The stench of the thing was obvious even when the door was closed, but up close it was incredible. Unlike the dead vicar, the flies had not touched this body, which only seemed odd to them afterwards, as though the priority of thoughts allowed only so much working memory at any one time. What was evident, despite the decay, was that this zombie had also been rendered safe.

"Immobilised," Larsen said, pointing at a stab wound in the neck as she covered her mouth and nose to inspect the body without touching it, "or at least a miss to the head."

Nobody answered for fear of having to draw in breath. They searched the house, satisfied that the only occupant was rotting in the room they were happy to shut off.

"In here," Enfield said, waiting for the others to join him. They weren't so unprofessional as to rush and make noise, and his call was made in a tone that didn't spark fear. The four of them found themselves looking at an open wardrobe with a solid metal cabinet with two keyholes, one high and one low, on display behind the rows of large shirts.

"Keys," Buffs whispered, and everyone cast out to magnify their search parameters for much smaller items. Each room was checked, every drawer and pot emptied for sign of the keys to allow them access to the gun cabinet. They all drew a blank until one last thought dawned on Johnson.

"In its pocket?" he said softly, seeing the disgust on at least one face. Larsen looked at the three men in turn, seeing no obvious sign of any of them volunteering for the task. Tutting loudly, she walked out and downstairs and into the kitchen, where she went straight to the under-sink cupboard to where she had seen what she needed. Pulling on a yellow washing-up glove, she strode towards the living room as she took a big gulp of a deep breath and walked in without breaking step. Slinging the gun behind her and bending down so as not to kneel in the leaking fluids coming from it, she thrust a hand into the trouser pockets of the corpse and let out a dry retch of disgust. Steadying herself and breathing into the crook of her elbow for a few beats, she repeated the process on the other side, until she jerked at the body and came out with a triumphant look on her pale face. Walking straight past them as they scattered, she thrust the gloved hand holding the keys into the sink and turned on the tap to rinse them of the greasy gore that covered them. She breathed hard, repaying the debt of oxygen to her body after holding her breath, and shook off the excess moisture into the sink before leading the way upstairs.

Johnson didn't know exactly what they were expecting, certainly not anything resembling the military hardware they all possessed, but somehow the two shotguns and one rifle still disappointed him. Enfield reached in to inspect the long gun, running his hands over it and feeling the weight and balance of the weapon as he tried to get to know it.

"This'll do," he said, reaching into the wardrobe again for

a padded gun slip and settling the new weapon inside. The boxes of bullets were handed out to him, as were the two empty magazines, which both held only five bullets each.

The two shotguns were also inspected, each placed into a similar carrying case and each with a large bag of ammunition to go with them. They were double-barrelled, but even two shots when you had none were better than nothing.

"Cut them down?" Buffs asked Johnson, "back-up weapons?"

Johnson nodded, thinking that nothing short of either platoon or company strength support weapons would be useful against more than a few of the things together, but that stealth was more sensibly employed. An army accustomed to war before the inception of firearms would fare better than the current model, he also thought, then looked down at the submachine gun in his hands, looking tiny in his grip, despite its fat barrel. He hadn't fired the thing yet, but he knew that there was no such thing as a silent weapon. Even the percussive cough it would make would be nothing compared to the ringing crack that the impacting round would make, but at least the sound shouldn't carry for miles like the booming report of a rifle. Or a shotgun.

With Johnson shaking himself out of his thoughts, they gladly escaped the smell of the house before moving on to the next one, taking only the salvaged weapons with them.

And that next house held items they were not expecting to find.

TWENTY-THREE

"Yes, Dezzy," Downes said comically as though talking to an eager child, "you can bring it."

"Woo," Dezzy said, playing the part, "thanks, Dad!" he said as he hefted the rescued GPMG and the belted ammunition to go with it, "can I have a go on the load-door gun too?"

Downes fixed him with a stern look which was still partly in character and glared at him until he folded. They had adopted a small ground floor room on one of the wings a short distance from the main entrance as their own. As was always the way with them, whatever part of whatever camp anywhere in the world they occupied, it became a kind of holy place that young soldiers stared at in awe, and others just pointedly ignored, unless they had cause to be there. As for the men themselves, even the Major, as they walked around without displaying any rank or insignia, they were often referred to as *'Oi, mate,'* by most regular soldiers. They dressed for war, putting on more layers and heavier clothing by necessity than the heat of the late summer made comfortable. Despite the warmth, none of the men was foolish or vain enough to wear short sleeves, and when they were finished, only the lack of black hoods pulled up and the anonymity of a full-face respirator made them look less the part than the iconic imagery of the embassy siege some nine years prior. That was the look that most people associated with their regiment; black-clad counter terrorist soldiers shrouded in mystery; but the truth was something wholly different.

When the younger Captain Downes had returned to his parent unit, the parachute regiment he still officially belonged to, as very few of the SAS were what was called permanent cadre, he was grilled by his peers about his experiences and found that all of them had entirely the wrong idea about the vaunted elite.

Officers were allowed to apply for selection, passing the same gruelling tests as any man, in addition to the planning exercises they had to complete, and if successful, they would serve a tour as a troop leader. That said, being the officer in charge of an SAS troop usually meant working for an experienced sergeant and listening to the more experienced soldiers under their technical command. After that, the young officers, Lieutenants and Captains, were returned to their units to develop and earn promotion. Even fewer were invited back for a second tour, but of those, only the absolute cream made it back as Majors to lead squadrons and hopefully perform well enough to be invited back for the last time as commanding officer. That was Clive Downes' career goal, once upon a time not too long before.

Col. Clive Downes. Commanding Officer 22 SAS. After that, who knew? A regimental posting back to the Paras as a colonel? A generalship? A UN or NATO command somewhere possibly, but he knew he certainly wouldn't be running around leading a four-man patrol of the toughest soldiers he had ever met.

Now that the world had gone to shit his career aspirations were dashed, but those were the last things on his mind. What was important to him were the lives of his men, the others around him and surviving the whole shit show. He turned to Mac and stood for the sergeant to check him over. The dour Scot was the only one of them to actually be permanently posted to their regiment, after years extending his attachment and making the dizzy heights of sergeant, and then leaving behind his original corporal rank when he left the Parachute Regiment years before. The others, Dez and Smiffy, were crap-hats, meaning that they had come from regiments that weren't prized for breeding the elite soldiers, unlike the parachute or rifle regiments. Who and what they were before hadn't really mattered to Downes even two months before, and it mattered even less so, now that they were the only ones of their regiment left that they knew of. Downes knew of the doomsday protocol, just as he knew of the various other members of the regiment who had been deployed to other parts of the world. If any of those postings became relevant, then he would say so, but for now, knowing that half of them were deployed to protect key European sites and routes from the risk of the Soviets capital-ising on the widespread panic didn't bode well for their overall numbers.

No, as much as he hated to admit it, they were among the last of their kind.

"Come on," Mac said, snapping him out of his dark reverie with a slap on the shoulder, "my turn."

Downes checked Mac's equipment, making sure nothing was loose and nothing rattled. He counted the magazines in the pouches of his webbing, totalling up the number of indi-vidual bullets at over two hundred. That might have seemed like a lot when looked at in the calm, cool daylight, but he knew from experience just how fast ammunition ran out. He liked to carry as much as was possible without hurting himself or compromising speed, because his only contacts with organ-ised sectarian criminals 'over the water' had led to a sudden and worrying lack of ammunition available. His memories of cowering in a soggy ditch, crawling a few yards and popping up to fire the magazine from his rifle in bursts before reloading and repeating, were vivid and unwelcome. Ever since the day he had finished his tour and returned to a maroon beret, he'd lobbied his own regiment to increase the standard ammunition issued to each man on active patrol, and each time the bureaucrats shot down his suggestions.

In the special forces he found the welcome rule-bending approach to such matters; if he or any of his men wanted a certain weapon or calibre for a particular deployment and could justify it, they got it. If they wanted new kit, more demolitions, then they requisitioned it and they got it. In the last requisitions they made,

the one for the barrow-load of 9mm rounds for their four MP5SDs as well as their pistols, they had also managed to get their hands on a pair of AA-12s.

As far as weaponry went, Downes knew these to be possibly the evillest things on the planet, with the possible exception of a bear trap. Both Mac and Dezzy carried one and they were the polar opposite to Smiffy's silent killer of a stolen Soviet sniper rifle. Both 12-bore shotguns were fully automatic, and both were loaded with an eight-round magazine. They also carried a replacement magazine in the form of a twenty-round drum, but the sheer size and bulk of them made it impossible to be carried as a back-up when equipped with the high-capacity load. Checking that it was secure, Downes recalled that Dezzy also carried one, along with the small demolitions pack and a few claymore anti-personnel mines. Along with the big machine gun and three belts of ammunition, Downes knew that he would be overloaded, even though he was the exact opposite of what people expected a special forces soldier to be. Dez wasn't a huge man, but his strength and stamina were like that of an ant and a goat that had been spliced in a laboratory. Even still, Downes wanted him unburdened.

"Dezzy, give me the shotgun. You're overloaded."

'Aww, come *on!*' Dezzy whined as though his commander was his father telling him that he couldn't bring a toy.

"So, the MP5, sidearm *and* gympy aren't enough for you? Are you planning on taking on the entire bloody zombie apocalypse by yourself? Don't be a twat; hand it over."

Dezzy glared for a second, his sullen face bordering on the belligerent as he removed the attitude only seconds before Downes would have an opinion on the matter. Dropping the kit in his hands, namely a large machine gun normally serviced by two men, he unslung and handed over the shotgun.

"I like to keep this handy," Dez said with a smirk and an appalling American accent, "for close encounters."

"Drum mag?" Downes asked, completely ignoring the *Aliens* quote and taking the gun. He reached out his other hand to receive it before turning to Mac and having him help add the extra armament to his back.

"We good?" Downes asked them, getting nods in return as the four of them filed out of their little den carrying enough firepower to start, or end, a small conflict.

————

The main pilot, Barrett, was his normal miserable self. Mac put that down to living in the pocket of his co-pilot, who permanently cracked jokes and quoted films, as well as the loadmaster, who was either asleep or else played music which, in a world where silence meant survival, seemed unwise.

Counterintuitive, I think is the word, Mac mused to himself, as was his way. He liked to find the longer words for everyday things as he believed a wider vocabulary made him more sophisticated. Separated him from the beasts. For a man who only spoke when he had to, a wider vocabulary seemed a wasteful hobby.

He glared at the two southerners, waiting for them to switch on and drop their constant clowning, which they always did the second it was time to concentrate. Downes stepped aboard the aircraft, followed by Smiffy, who turned to reach out a hand to take the heavy machine gun from his friend, who then climbed up himself. Mac took one long, lingering panoramic view of the inside of the huge square and the inner courtyard.

"Mac," Downes shouted, raising his voice again as the whining noise of the starting engines ramped up, "let's go."

"Aye," Mac replied to himself, "still got a bad feeling about this one," and climbed up into the Sea King.

The flight to Yeovilton took less than half an hour and their arrival was marked by a slowing of their air speed and a looping, banking manoeuvre to allow a clear view of the area.

"Fence is down in a few places," Morris' voice came through the headset from the cockpit, "looks like the base was trampled from north to south a while ago."

"Any sign of movement?" Mac asked just as Downes' mouth opened to say the same thing. The two men's eyes met, both waiting for the answer to crackle into their ears over the deafening whine of the engines and rotor blades. That pause stretched on almost reassuringly; reassuringly in the sense that the immediate answer wasn't an affirmative, and also reassuring in that the man was obviously looking and not giving some half-arsed answer which could put them in danger.

"Nothing moving," Morris said in a clear, flat tone.

"Okay, put us down as close to the refuelling point as possible," Downes said as he put an automatic hand to the boom mic attached to his headset and unclipped his belt to rise, "swing by and show me the landing site," he said as he gripped on tight and leaned his head around to look out of the open side door.

The pilot took them around, slowing almost to a static hover as Brinklow pointed straight down to a rank of large fuel tanks. Downes called into the headset that he had seen it and that they should take them in to land. He turned to face his team and gave instructions, "One-eighty cover. Push out twenty and drop; Dezzy centre with the gympy," he finished, putting the biggest firepower, that of the GPMG in the hands of his demolitions man, in the middle of their small defence so as to give it the best arc of fire available. He didn't need to add that they should keep it as quiet as possible unless forced to go loud by numbers they couldn't deal with easily.

They all unstrapped, readied themselves and hung on tight as the wheels bumped into the tarmac to signify that they should jump down. Their legs bent under the excess weight of their gear and armaments, and then forced themselves straight again to make them upright through sheer power and strength of will. Fanning out to cover the side from where a threat could come, the four men rested into position and kept their senses fully alert over the sights of their guns. Their senses of sound and smell were useless, as behind them the stink of hot oil and exhaust gases swirled around under the deafening rotor wash, and forced them to use sight alone as Brinklow rushed around with Morris to refuel the helicopter.

Their concentration was such that the refuelling was completed in a time which seemed too short, but Brinklow was tapping Downes on the shoulder before cupping his hands between his own mouth and the Major's ear.

"Refuelled," he yelled over the noise of the engines ramping up again, "small arms locker in there if you want it?" he shouted, pointing to a nearby single-storey building which had the appearance of a guard station. Downes nodded, turning and running low to Mac to use hand signals to indicate he should follow him. He tried to catch the eyes of the others, but their position and concentration was such that he had to jog the distances to both of them and repeat the process of giving hand signals for them to redeploy and cover the helicopter with just the two of them.

Brinklow followed Downes and Mac at a respectful distance so as to stay well away from any contact that might present itself.

The two soldiers stacked up on the door and Downes waited for Mac's hand to rest on his shoulder before placing his left hand on the door handle and turning it. Letting the door swing open a fraction, he fought against the natural urge to reach to his chest and throw in a flashbang to stun anyone in the room; instead, he pushed the door wide and called out a hello to see if anyone or anything inside moved.

Nothing.

The ambient noise of the nearby helicopter still drowned out any chance of detecting the slight sounds of small movement, so he went in to clear the room. Mac followed, going right to Downes' left as their gun barrels swung left and right, always pointing in the direction of their eyes. Two doors came off the main room and they were cleared similarly, resulting in the posture of both men relaxing as they stood tall and lowered their guns.

"Weapons locker," Brinklow said, pointing to a badly painted wooden cupboard of a size and design that appeared out of place, "and ammunition," he said, indicating a heavy lock box underneath a desk secured with a heavy padlock.

Downes opened the tall cupboard, finding the contents to be a squad's worth of new personal arms. Eight SA80 rifles and a longer, bigger version called the LSW, or light support weapon, which was effectively a smaller calibre version of the heavier GPMG machine guns. The LSW was significantly more man-portable than the older GPMGs, or just a longer-barrelled version of the SA80, however you chose to view them. A locking bar ran through the rack, preventing the weapons from being removed, which was secured with another bar, far smaller than the one on the lock box, and Downes turned to Mac.

"Dezzy got a cutting torch in his dems kit?"

Mac shrugged, turning to the door and checking the outside before jogging across the open expanse towards the helicopter.

Downes saw Mac take the big machine gun, kneeling down to settle behind it, as Dez ran back to the helicopter and reappeared with a black rucksack which he shrugged into, and jogged towards the building. That rucksack, the team's demolitions kit, was usually condensed for whatever option they had, but having the helicopter to carry them, Dezzy had added everything he could find to cater for their needs.

"What do you need, Boss?" he asked as he strode in. In answer, Downes pointed at the locking bar and the heavy padlock on the metal box under the counter. Dez nodded, dropped the bag and rummaged for a set of heavy bolt croppers. The tool made short work of the smaller lock, with only the strength of the man's arms needing to be employed. Snapping the lock away, he knelt and began to work on the far thicker metal of that padlock, making difficult crimps into the bar at intervals before dropping the tool and reaching into his kit to spark up the small gas cutting torch he carried. Downes knew that without a far larger gas tank, the tool wasn't going to last for long, but it didn't have to. Even such a small prize of a few hundred rounds of 5.56 was worth the effort, so Dez worked the torch into the gap where he had cut crimps into the metal, killing the torch to snatch up the croppers before the metal cooled too much. He sat down and brought up his knees to brace one arm of the tool against his knees, with both hands on the furthest arm away.

A grunt built up low in his belly, building into a growl of massive effort as the long arms of the tools flexed, before a muted click sounded. Relaxing, he prised the tool open again and used his gloved hands to swivel the hot remains of the lock and remove it before shaking his hand at the radiating heat.

"Good to go," he said, looking up at Downes with a smile and breathing hard from the effort.

"Then let's get gone."

CHAPTER

TWENTY-FOUR

In some bizarre mirror occurrence of the last time Peter had been inside a house when it was broken into, he grabbed the girl and bundled her ahead of him into the airing cupboard. To her credit, she never once resisted him and never once made a single sound; she understood the importance of speed and silence. Throwing himself inside on top of spare sheets and towels as he had done before, he cursed himself as he remembered leaving his camouflage backpack and pitchfork on the rug at the end of the bed where they had been when the noises began. Panicking at the lack of reassurance of having the shotgun in his sweaty grip or the trusted 'sticker' of his pitchfork, his grip found the backup spike and held tight to it.

The wood of the front door frame cracked and splintered and the muffled sounds of boots on carpet echoed up the stairs to where the crack of light came through to their hiding place. Amber's hand sought desperately in the dark for his and their fingers interlocked tightly, and although Peter wanted to keep two hands ready to use the only weapon at his disposal, he could not bring himself to let her go.

Muffled voices, spoken low and not whispered, carried

inarticulately up the stairs to where he hid, but they gave no clues as to who or what they were.

They're alive, he told himself, *not that it makes them any less dangerous.*

His thoughts were interrupted by footsteps, louder now as they combined with the creaks of the stairs and the banging of his own pulse thudding in his ears to drown out the minute details. He breathed steadily, trying to force his heartrate to slow down, and failing.

When it was just him, before he was responsible for Amber, he would have allowed his fear to dominate him and take over, but now, with another life which he saw as more important than his own, he steeled himself and prepared to fight.

They aren't taking her, too, he swore to himself, *I'm not losing someone else.*

Just as he thought this, two soft clicks grabbed his attention. Peering into the gap of the door and trying to interpret the slight shifting of shadows, Peter tried to make sense of what he was hearing and tried even harder to keep his rapid breathing quiet.

———

Johnson took his turn using the crowbar on the door. While not as overtly muscular as Bufford, his longer limbs and height advantage made him very strong. Bufford had the stocky look of a power-lifter, whereas Johnson just looked *big*.

The door came open easily and the second two behind him made their entry. Buffs and Astrid moved fluidly, working as a well-drilled pair who had no intrinsic link of training together, although their efficiency spoke of hours drilling from the same manual. They cleared the downstairs rapidly and effectively, muttering to the other two who had filed in to adopt defensive stances, then pointed out a small, wheeled truck loaded with food cans and packets enough to sustain a person for a few days. Nodding to Bufford, Astrid took the lead as she climbed the stairs quietly, freezing near the top of the stairs at a soft double click of the SBS man's fingers. She glanced back briefly to see where he was pointing. Her eyes followed the line of his outstretched finger to fall on the strange double-pronged spear propped against a bedroom wall and a battered green camouflage rucksack below with the obvious grip of a modified, sawn-off shotgun protruding from the opening. Astrid and Buffs locked eyes, retreating a few paces down the stairs to give themselves space.

"What's going on?" Johnson asked softly as they stepped carefully backwards whilst keeping their eyes on the top of the stairs.

Buffs came down first, cupping his hand and placing his mouth close enough to Johnson's face for his beard to catch in the SSM's stubble.

"Signs of someone holed-up," he muttered, "weapons and equipment."

Johnson pulled back and regarded him, looking at Larsen, who kept her eyes glued to the top of the stairs with her gun raised. Deciding what to do in a heartbeat, Johnson stepped forward to the foot of the stairs and called out in a powerful but unthreatening voice.

"Hello? We don't mean any harm, I assure you…" he said, turning an ear towards the stairs to listen intently for any sound in response. He heard nothing.

"We're from the British Army," he announced, ignoring the fact it that what he had said applied only to himself, "and we know you're up there. We are just looking for supplies," he explained, not bothering to say that they were clearing the village to make it safer, "and we won't hurt you or try to take what you have."

Still no response, so he waited.

———

As soon as the deep voice rang out from downstairs, Amber's fingers dug into Peter's hand and her breathing doubled in panicked intensity. He squeezed her hand back, trying to convey through touch that it was okay and that he wouldn't let anyone hurt her, just as the words the big, deep voice of the man used wormed into his brain.

They're army, he thought with sudden elation, *but if they really are from the army why aren't there more of them? Where are their tanks?*

As these conflicting thoughts bounced around his head the voice called out again.

"I'm coming upstairs," it said loud and clear, but careful and somehow soft at the same time, "I'm not going to hurt anyone, you have my word."

Both Peter and Amber were breathing hard now, and the boy's sweaty grip tightened in waves on the spike gripped in his hand as his pulse surged through his adrenaline-flooded body. The footsteps sounded, louder this time, and making Peter think of a giant bearing down on them. He had nothing left to do, nowhere to go, and for the briefest of moments he became the scared child he had been before everything in the world had changed.

Screwing his eyes shut tightly, he pretended that he wasn't there, as though the childish belief would protect him. When the footsteps stopped outside the door to the airing cupboard and a large shadow passed by, Peter felt a coolness descend on him. His breathing became controlled, his senses sharpened, and his body stopped trembling. He didn't understand the physiological responses to adrenaline, but he didn't need to; his body was saturated with the natural drug, and he levelled out at the point where he was in the most total control of himself he had ever been. Eyes narrowing, he shook his hand free of

Amber's, kicked his feet out to open the door and dropped onto the carpeted landing in one movement. His body had faced the choice of fight or flight, and his body had chosen the former.

———

Johnson, his hands up and open and the gun dangling just above his waist and bouncing gently from leg to leg, bypassed the airing cupboard in favour of clearing the bedrooms first, and froze as a sound behind him ripped the air. The sound made him think that it was involuntary, as though the person making it was simply so scared or angry that it came out of their mouth unintentionally. He whipped around, hands reaching for the grip of the weapon instinctively, but abandoning the move and making to raise his hands again. He stood up straight again after having moved into a crouch when threatened by the noise, when he saw his attacker.

The boy was unkempt, even if he was clean. His hair was too long and scruffy, the clothes he wore were ill-fitting and obviously scavenged, and in his hand was what looked like a home-made ice pick. The boy drew back his teeth in an animalistic snarl of rage and raised the weapon like the shower scene in *Psycho*.

Johnson reached out, grasped the wrist as easily as if he were picking flowers, and plucked the weapon from the weak hand as though no resistance was offered. He kept hold of the wrist, not gripping it painfully but holding on enough that the boy was on tiptoes and off balance and spoke to him.

"It's okay," he growled over the effort of dangling the feral child, "it's okay. I'm not going to hurt you."

The boy grunted with the effort of trying to break free, reaching up with his left hand to try and prise open the fingers as wide as sausages and as tough as leather. He even tried to haul himself up to bite the hand, but lacked the reach. Johnson tried patience, but his aching body and lack of experience at having his instructions ignored snapped something inside of him.

"That's e-bloody '*nuff!*" he barked, seeing the boy freeze and stare at him, "we're not here to hurt you, I said, now *pack this in*," he continued in only a fractionally softer tone before lifting the boy slightly and releasing his grip to see him fall down to the carpet.

The boy spun and fixed him with a look of rage, then the eyes seemed to change. They lost their murderous fiery intensity and flashed instantly glossy to show where the tears pricked at him. Johnson didn't know if it was anger, fear or even relief but the sight of it made him soften.

———

Peter's sudden aggression abandoned him as quickly as it had taken over. The man wasn't a monster, and he wasn't one of the ones who had dragged away Amber's mother.

He doesn't look like one of them, anyway, he thought.

His claims to be from the army seemed true enough, as the man wore the right equipment and had rank badges on his sleeves, and something about his equipment made Peter feel certain that it was well-worn even before everything started. The man spoke to him again, more calmly this time, and repeated that he wasn't going to hurt him. He seemed to deflate as he spoke, seemed to get smaller and appear less threatening, like he was changing modes or something.

"What's your name, son?" he asked.

Peter, sat on the floor, looking up at the huge man who he realised was bigger, *much* bigger than his father, and for some reason, he couldn't make his mouth work to form words. Noises behind him made him jolt, and he saw two more faces on the staircase; one bearded and wild and the other angular, fair and framed by blonde hair tied up loosely. He turned back to the first man and found his voice.

"You promise?" he croaked, throat dry from the adrenaline.

"We promise," answered the blonde woman in a voice that sounded strange to Peter's ears, "we won't hurt you."

At the sound of her voice a stifled cry came out of the partly open airing cupboard and all eyes except Peter's shot to stare at the gap. He slowly rose up from the floor, fearfully regressing weeks to worry that being in close proximity to adults would result in renewed casual violence towards his small body, and he switched his anxious gaze between them as he reached back inside their hiding place.

"It's okay," he said softly over the muffled sounds of protesting squeaks, "it's okay, come on."

Peter half pulled, half helped her out of the slatted wooden shelf and heard gasps from behind him. She came out, gripping her small arms around his neck and burying her face into his neck so as not to see the new people they had run from.

"I'm Peter," he said quietly as he stared at one spot on the wall to overcome his conflicting feelings of defeat and relief, "and this is Amber."

"Is she your sister?" the big man asked him gently.

"No," Peter said, turning to look at him and wrongly direct some pent-up anger in his direction, "she was left alone after people broke into a house and took her mum away," he said in a tone that sounded like more of an accusation than he intended. His eyes stayed glued to the man's, watching the anger and indignation mirrored in his face, and communication something verging on mutual happened between them.

"Come downstairs with us?" the woman said in her curious voice, "and tell us what happened?"

They did. Peter collected his weapons and bag from where

he had left them and none of the others tried to take them from him. They sat down, giving the children space and time to relax around them, but Peter's eyes were constantly drawn to their weapons. He checked them all in turn; the big man he had first tried to attack with his spike, the bearded man who might have looked like a circus strong man if he hadn't been dressed in black and carrying weapons; the tall and almost ghostly man who was much younger than the other males who had broken in to their hiding place, and who seemed to drift instead of moving, even with the massive rifle slung over his back like some kind of Robin Hood. He unnerved Peter a little, but he got the impression that he and Amber unnerved the man in return.

What surprised the boy was Amber's behaviour; she had emerged from his neck with a red, wet face to stare at the blonde woman and wear a strange hint of a smile.

"My name is Squadron Sergeant Major Johnson," the big man said before he seemed to wince and decide to start again, "my name is Dean."

Peter nodded at him.

"This is Sergeant Bufford," he said as he indicated the bearded man and realised that he knew nothing else about him other than his unit.

"Alex, but call me Buffs," the beard said, cracking in half with a smile.

"This is Marine Enfield," Johnson went on as he gestured towards the younger man, "he's a sniper."

Peters eyes went wide with boyish adoration, but he quicker contained himself.

"And I am Astrid," said the woman before she could be introduced. At the sound of her voice Amber tensed a little, turning back into Peter's neck. Interpreting her reaction to mean that she wanted to know more about the woman, Peter asked her a question.

"Are you in the army too?" he asked, having taken in her equipment and sensed something about her mannerism that said she was indeed some kind of soldier.

"Yes, but in the armed forces of Norway. Do you know where that is?" she responded. Peter shook his head.

"Go to the top of Scotland," Enfield interrupted with a small smile and the bitterness of a marine forced to train for arctic warfare in sub-zero temperatures, "turn right and stop when you've found the coldest place on earth."

"Ah, so you have been to my country?" Astrid responded gently with a chuckle.

The conversation stalled until Johnson spoke again.

"I think we've accidentally taken over your house, Peter," he said, seeing the answer clearly on the boy's face, "and eaten some of your supplies, not counting what you had in the cart ready to go. Very clever that, by the way."

Peter smiled at the compliment despite himself, giving him the confidence to ask a question of his own.

"Did you use all of the hot water?"

Guilty glances among the four newcomers confirmed that they had.

"It's okay," Peter said, "it's sunny so it will fill up soon."

"Solar panels?" Astrid asked, "I didn't think you had them here yet?"

"Yes," Peter told her before changing the subject, "so do you have a camp or something?"

More glances bounced around the room until Johnson spoke again.

"We did have, twice actually," he said in a low voice, "but we got separated after a helicopter crash. A lot of people…" he trailed off after a subtle throat-clearing noise from Astrid, "a lot of people didn't make it. There are two more of us, another man and another woman, in the other house. Will you come back with us?"

Peter looked at Amber, who stared right back at him and shrugged her little shoulders as if to say that it was his call. That he could decide their fate. That the boy who had such a biologically ingrained fear of adults could choose for not only himself but for her, too.

If it hadn't been for her, if he hadn't thought that he could provide for her and keep her safe, he probably would have chosen differently.

CHAPTER

TWENTY-FIVE

The flight over the island was a depressing one. Hundreds of zombies wandered around looking for anything to spark their interest. Morris' focus was drawn inexorably out of the cockpit window towards what could only have been one of the faster ones wearing a blood-blackened military uniform and making leap after desperate leap at a small flock of white gulls. They evaded the jumps easily, always flapping their wings and skipping clear of the lunging attacks to disperse and dart back to peck at the food source they were unwilling to give up. Feathers swirled around the display, making it clear that at least one of them hadn't been quick enough or lucky enough.

The island was totally overrun, teeming with Screechers and making any attempt to rescue the ammunition or fuel left there simply too dangerous. Worse still, there was no sign of the helicopter there. Following the flight path they had done on so many relay trips previously, Barrett moved the helicopter at less than half the speed he had before to allow more eyes to cover more ground. Morris pointed ahead and far off course to their right, indicated a lazy spire of wispy, black smoke for Barrett to wordlessly bank the aircraft and point the bulbous nose in that direction. A little over a minute later they were in a hover at a hundred feet up, looking down on the charred and twisted remains of their sister helicopter, which had merged with the scorched stone of the church it had crashed into. Bodies were strewn around the wreckage, one of them being fed on by a young man wearing filthy blue jeans and a torn shirt as he craned his neck up to reach for the spinning machine far out of his grasp.

They turned away, the tail of the aircraft spinning around, to aim their nose in the direction of the base, and dipped forwards to leave the site of the crash without noticing the trail leading away through the long grass. Their heading led them directly towards another pillar of smoke.

The base, even after the daylight horror of the island and the crash site, made their hearts drop in their chests. The side of the base, which had been previously untouched, with the exception of a couple of downed sections of fencing, now looked like a burning, wrecked ant farm. Screechers pinged aimlessly about, pulled in all directions by the sounds and smells of the recent warzone to have erupted there. The building containing the vehicles pulsed thick smoke out of the large hangar doors and all around there were smears of blood, scorched patches of ground and groups of zombies feeding on the bodies of those too far destroyed to turn and join the ranks of the enemy. Silence reigned inside the helicopter, even as the SAS men leaned out of the doors to look at the horrors below. Barrett eventually decided that they had seen enough and turned to head for their new base.

Flying slowly and not too high, Brinklow looked out of the side door in a daze. One hand rested on the fixed gun and one gripped the fuselage as his brain tried to make sense of what he had seen. There were no answers, at least none that explained the obvious carnage, and his rage grew with each feature that blurred by below him. He could feel himself building up with each tree or building that passed until the shambling, loping line of corpses he saw in one field finally made him snap.

"Slow it down," he called into the mic savagely, hauling back on the action of the gun and bending into it. The helicopter slowed, and he began to go to work on the rearmost zombies in the group, cutting them down with efficient bursts of fire. He fired four, five, six bursts with the last one cutting down a small knot of three. They all appeared to be moving in the same direction with purpose; no deviation or wandering off after wildlife or other distractions, and just as Brinklow pointed the barrel ahead, he understood why.

"Fuck me," he shouted, startling them all, "get ahead of these bastards and set her down. Now!" he yelled. At the tone of his voice the SAS men sparked into life, not knowing what, but still knowing that something would require their attention. Barrett complied, not focusing on what Brinklow was shooting at as he battled his own dark thoughts, but now he surged ahead and swung the tail around to show the open side door to the advancing line of enemy.

"Come on!" Brinklow shouted, waving desperately as the beleaguered soldier staggered forwards near the point of collapse. That was what Brinklow had seen, they now knew, the Screechers were following a meal and had so very nearly caught up to their running buffet. The ones trailing back were the slower ones, but the faster ones, the *Limas*, were so close behind him that he could probably smell them.

Brinklow found himself pushed bodily aside by Dezzy, who made an exaggerated hand gesture whilst shouting, "Drop! Get Down!"

The soldier understood, throwing himself face-first flat into the long grass. As he did, Dez unleashed a torrent of automatic fire at head height just where he had been a fraction of a second before. The three faster ones, who were no fewer than ten paces behind the man and gaining, were decapitated in a flash, their heads erupting in clouds of pink mist as their life-less, or more appropriately inanimate, bodies dropped like sacks of potatoes.

"Come on!" Brinklow roared, having moved around the machine gun to stand in the open doorway as the man struggled to his feet and half fell the remaining distance to safety. Brinklow grabbed both of his outstretched arms and hauled for all he was worth, sliding the man bodily about as he shouted, "Up! Up!" into the mic. The pilot responded, the aircraft surged sickeningly into the sky, and they were away.

"Hey!" the loadmaster shouted in the man's face as another headset was forced over his ears, "What the fuck happened?" The man's eyes fluttered, and his answers came with the heavy expulsion of each laboured breath. He had clearly been running for miles, pursued every step of the way until random chance conspired with fate to save him.

"Attacked," he gasped, "whole fucking… herd of them… in a building…"

"So what happened?" Brinklow snapped.

"Fucking… Nevin…" the man said, "bastard left us… there to… die."

CHAPTER

TWENTY-SIX

"Let's go then," Sinclair said, his voice sounding weak to Nevin in his intentionally chosen position of the least responsibility and danger. He ran forward with them, never pushing to the front or dropping to the back in case they were attacked. He hung back tactically, again to avoid anything resembling hard work, as the stiff handles employed to wind open the hangar doors were ratcheted around to inch open those doors bit by bit. Nevin cowered in cover, protected by everyone and never placing himself in a position where he would have to fight. As soon as the doors were open enough, he let three others slip through the gap first as the handles were continually wound for the gap to grow wider. When no sounds of alarm or gunfire came from inside, he slipped out of the sunshine and into the cool, dark interior lit only by the weak bulb lining the walls above head height. He blinked and let out an involuntary shiver at the change of environment.

"Nevin," snapped the voice of a corporal, "don't just stand there like a fucking ornament; get working, you bellend!"

Nevin's hand slipped inside the pocket where the old revolver sat, touching it briefly for reassurance before he ran off to start working; only his agenda was different. He planned to get himself alone in a vehicle and as soon as they were out of there, he would break away and do his own thing. He would desert from the army, what was left of it, and he would never look back.

Searching the area nearest the door for something appropriate, his eyes rested on the small, low-to-the ground profile of a Ferret. This was the kind of thing that the big bastard Johnson would normally kick around in with a radio operator and driver. The thing looked like a smaller version of their Fox cars which Nevin usually drove, only this was one of the rare enclosed versions with a turret. His teeth flashed white in the low light as a smile spread across his face, looking at the turret which housed a mounted thirty-calibre machine gun. Climbing up and flipping open the hatch, he lowered himself inside to reach for the fuel pump and ignition switches, before hitting the starter button to bark the Rolls Royce engine into life.

All around him, other engines were sparking into similar life as Nevin juddered the little scout car forward and out into the sunlight. The mission was a two-stage thing, because the vehicles on their own were only so useful without the ammunition to equip them. The obvious logic of the British Army dictated that the two elements would be stored in different places, so the requirement was to collect vehicles and then move to the ammunition dump to equip them, and Nevin didn't want to turn his coat before he had some bullets for the heavy machine gun above him.

———

The raised voice of Sergeant Sinclair sparked a sequence of events that led to devastation. All of the trapped zombies inside came to life in a weirdly organic way as the few nearest the wall where the sound came from began to animate and moan as they hissed air in through their noses to try and detect the source. That excitement spread like a rumour, with zombies eight or nine bodies back from the source mimicking the animation of the others without knowing why, until within a minute, every one of the dormant monstrosities was riled up and moaning and bumping into one another. The cacophony they raised went unnoticed by the people who had awoken them as the growling engines masked the sound of impending horror.

One of the zombies, late to the party as one of the last to be infected by the unexplained excitement, sparked into animated hissing and movement until another one, far bigger, collided with her as she was off balance. It flew backwards and fell, slamming its narrow shoulders into a horizontal bar on a door, clicking open the lock and swinging the door wide. The suddenly louder sounds of engines filled the building, making the noise level roll and rise in intensity as the remnants of the swarm began to surge towards the noise and crush together to escape through the open door. The one who had freed them, albeit inadvertently, never regained her feet as the horde trampled over her. The sounds of crunching and cracking bones were nearly inaudible over the hissing and groaning, as were the sickening squelches of her body being flattened by each footfall. The first twenty bodies to step over her made it impossible for her to mobilise again and regain her feet. The next twenty flattened her entirely, leaving only her skull and snapping teeth moving as other bodies tripped over her to fall and suffer the same fate, before her lower jaw was dislocated and half removed by a heavy boot. The last thing her cloudy eye saw before she was snuffed out entirely was a single point of a high-heeled shoe descending into her eye socket to puncture the brain and stick there, tripping the wearer slightly to stagger over her skull and leave her to her final rest as a greasy smear fanning out from the open doorway.

The remnants of the swarm poured their exodus into the open with renewed animation, heading for the sounds of life.

———

"Everybody load up," Sinclair said, repeating his order to his left and right as he waved his free hand towards the six fighting vehicles and small fuel tanker. The men providing cover ran to comply, dropping their lower bodies into hatches and keeping their eyes alert over the sights of their weapons. The journey to the ammunition store was a short one, and to speed their progress Sinclair ordered the gates and fences to be driven through by the lead vehicle; a replacement Spartan for Maxwell's Assault Troop.

Nevin, again near enough in the middle of the procession to maximise his survival chances, followed the rear of the wagon in front and felt the nervous anticipation rise inside him. He would break away soon, somehow, and he would be free of them.

Maybe I'll even go back and find better stuff, he thought to himself, imagining the spoils of scavenging when unchecked by the stifling discipline of the army, before thinking of the spoils which could be found elsewhere. All he needed was somewhere he could hide away, somewhere with plenty of food and drink – above all he craved to drink – and wait out the whole mess until rescue came and he could worm back into life as though nothing had happened.

He'd claim that he was cut off, obviously, say that he'd bravely sought the rest of his squadron but assumed them all lost. He lapsed into something resembling a daydream as he drove slowly through the camp, with his wheels intermittently rattling over a downed gate or tangled mess of fencing.

Arriving at the ammo dump, he climbed out, mindful that his was the only vehicle not to require the 7.62 or 30mm rounds, and knowing also that he couldn't trust his ability to bully or intimidate anyone else into doing his heavy lifting this time. He found what he needed, dragging two large boxes of the heavy thirty-calibre bullets out to beside his small scout car, and prised the wooden casing open with his bayonet to rest it on the roof, before climbing back up and inside to load the first belt into the turret weapon.

Because of the sounds of engines, he didn't hear the first shouts of alarm. He didn't notice the running men fleeing for the safety of the building or their new vehicles. Instead, the first sign he saw of anything being wrong was when he popped his head back out of the hatch and saw a grey-skinned, mottled corpse

standing on the roof of the Spartan, holding a man up by his webbing straps. Nevin watched in terrible slow-motion as the arms contracted, muscles bunching against the weight of the struggling soldier, and the open mouth met the upcoming neck as the man pumped desperately with his bayonet to uselessly puncture the abdomen and chest of his attacker. The zombie bit down, tearing warm flesh and rupturing blood vessels as it tore a chunk away and chewed to spill hot swathes of bright, red blood over itself.

———

As the crowd exiting the building lost momentum due to the dilution of the noises outside, the change in pitch and tone of the engine sounds as the small convoy drove away served to focus them once more. Rounding the building into sight of where the people had been only moments before, their heads turned to stare in the direction of the fading noise. As one, with a single mind and common purpose, the horde surged in that direction as though they were a flock of birds in flight.

As was always the way, the faster ones pushed their way

through the mass to lead from the front, and they pushed out ahead of the more common, slower variety. This sparked the followers to push harder to catch up with the leaders, as if they somehow knew that these special ones, these messiahs, would lead them towards food. They walked through damaged fences and ruined gateways, increasing their pace with every step towards the growing sounds, until they rounded a ninety-degree bend and saw their prize. And again, as one, they attacked.

———

Nevin froze, not knowing what to do for the briefest of moments. The irony of his position was totally lost on him; for a man who hated being told what to do, he didn't realise that his brain was waiting for precisely that to happen and he lost valuable time until his brain forced a reaction. Men ran in all directions as gunfire rang out. They were disorganised, caught out in the open, and only one of them had already loaded a large enough weapon to stem the tide of incoming monsters.

Had Nevin been switched on, had he thought about anyone but himself, then he would have advanced the scout car thirty metres, climbed back and up into the turret, and degraded the attack with automatic fire from his heavy machine gun. The thirty-calibre bullets at that range would slice through so much dead flesh and kill five or six of them with each round, but he didn't act. Didn't do what he should to protect the lives of a dozen other men, each of whom was laying down his lives for the sake of others.

Nevin didn't think like that. He thought for himself. He acted out of fear and self-interest.

Instead of driving towards the danger to rescue the situation, which was not yet lost, he slammed the Ferret into reverse and blasted away in a growling roar of exhaust noise until he was far removed from the danger. He froze again, not being aware of his position in the camp relative to any known escape route, and he climbed back into the turret to better see his surroundings. His hands on the controls of the gun, he swivelled the turret to find a way out before his eyes rested on the few bodies loping towards him at something resembling a drunken jog. Unthinkingly, and ignoring all lessons of fire safety and weapon discipline he had ever received, he opened fire on them, spraying bullets in undisciplined clouds instead of concentrating them in bursts to achieve his objective. Behind the attackers, exposed in the open and almost overrun, were the rest of the men of Sinclair's detachment. The bullets from Nevin's wild firing did indeed cut down his attackers, even though his fire served only to disable the majority and not render them safe, but it also stitched into the only semblance of ordered defence around the vehicle Sinclair had occupied, and it had done so just as one of his men was aiming one of their Carl Gustav shoulder-mounted rockets.

The man knelt behind the tentative cover of a Fox, aiming for the main mass of the attack coming at them, and his shot would probably have scattered and ruined twenty or more of the leading ranks of enemy, to give them at least a scrap of a chance of survival. Instead, a single thirty-calibre bullet entered his body and shattered his right hip, spinning him distortedly to land on his left side with his head turned towards the open doors of the ammunition dump.

The rocket fired, showing a huge back-blast and issuing an echoing *boom* of a high-powered rifle which was precisely what the weapon was. The heavy round flew unseen through the doors, puncturing the thin metal skin of walls to detonate against a heavy steel locker containing the smokescreen bombs. Those smoke screens were the worst thing to have been hit, as the heat and force of the impact ignited the white phosphorous inside to raise the temperature inside the metal cabinet to an impossibly high level. The rest of the white phosphorous also caught fire, bursting thick, white smoke through the cracks in the cabinet and distorting the metal with the heat until it began to sag and melt. The ammunition stacked and stored nearby, ready to load into the vehicles, suffered from the heat and began to 'cook off' as the accelerant charge inside their casings heated sufficiently to fire their projectiles. Each explosion caused another, until the air was filled with the sound of a fire-work show from hell as rounds of all calibres blew until they combined to create a seemingly endless detonation that shook the ground and crushed Nevin's eardrums even through the sealed armour of his wagon.

Scrambling back down to the driving seat, he threw it into gear again and drove hard away from the rolling thunder to crash through fences and bump over the uneven ground.

He laughed desperately, almost maniacally as he drove away, his laughter lapsing and devolving into bursts of sobbing and tears, before the laughter broke through again. It was the final shred of decency in his body being forced out; exorcised by his cowardice and cruel, selfish nature.

———

Only one other man survived the swarming zombies and savage explosions on the base. Having been on the wrong, or perhaps in hindsight *right* side of the building when the attack was first detected, Trooper Povey faced a choice not dissimilar to Nevin's. Even though most of the detachment were from Sinclair's unit and he belonged to Maxwell's Assault Troop, the men under attack were still his, regardless of who their boss was. Povey knew that they were all one, and his true nature showed as he ran towards the fight and not away from it.

As he ran, the air from his right punched at his senses as heavy bullets pounded past. He ducked away instinctively, hitting the rough ground and rolling to retreat from the fire, which he traced from the broken bodies of a knot of Screechers back to the source. Seeing the dull green of the Ferret and wasting half a second as his brain registered the sheer rarity of finding a turreted version instead of the normal open-top variant, he looked back to his left as the huge booming sound echoed out. Seconds later came the crackling, shattering reports of ammunition cooking off, yet still Povey forced himself to his feet to run towards his men, just as the first blossoming fireballs and screaming sounds of tortured ricochets rang out. Another blast knocked him back down and focused his brain, but only sparked him into movement when a stream of zombies lined up their sights on him and began to advance.

Povey ran.

He ran out of the base and across country, fighting with uneven footing and a gathering chase every step of the way. He managed to keep ahead of the pursuit, only just, having paused twice to unload the last two magazines for his submachine gun to thin the ranks of the pack on his heels. Exhaustion, dehydration and fear boiled his senses into total panic, which served only to keep his legs moving. Every step he took threatened to be fractionally slower than the last until he knew with absolute certainty that he would eventually fall. Weird memories filed through his head in non-chronological order, having no relevance to the situation and making no sense to him, until one memory seemed more vivid than the others. It was the memory of a GPMG firing, and the feel of a helicopter's rotor wash overhead, until the aircraft in his imagination descended before him and a man screamed at him to get down.

TWENTY-SEVEN

Nevin drove until his panic abated. He didn't know how far or how hard he had driven, but he was certain that his inability to make choices had led him in any path other than one heading directly away from the camp.

His first realisation of this was when his foot hit the brakes in response to what his eyes were seeing, but his mind hadn't told him he had recognised yet. He found himself on a grass hill with deep swathes of chalk-coloured rock protruding from the small tussocks where stiff, long grass sprouted up to sway in the breeze.

He sat and stared out of the driver's small viewing window at what he realised with dawning reality was the sea. Far, far in the distance to the south, the horizon seemed to hold a dark, almost storm-like quality which would have given any person capable of rational thought a feeling of foreboding. Nevin felt no such warning, despite his knowledge of what had happened on the continent to cause such devastation as could be seen over the less than thirty-mile distance, and instead he worked the gears to reverse the scout car and drive more carefully back down the slope to find a road. Amid the bumps and squeaks inside his hot tin can, he continued to laugh to himself, only now it came as sporadic chuckles, sounding as though he had recalled something mildly amusing.

He drove through a low fence, not appearing to even notice it, and stopped at the side of the tarmac, where even after the short time since the dead had started eating people, the land had started to show the first signs of becoming overgrown. Deciding that he couldn't see enough of the road either way to make an informed decision, he flipped open the hatch to drive with his head protruding, choosing to turn right for no good reason.

He rolled along the roads, almost forgetting the horrors he had endured over the last month and slowly allowed his senses and wits to fully return to him. One of those senses he retained was smell, and the acrid stench of the dried urine in the fabric of his uniform trousers wafted up to pass his nose and eyes as it was blasted away in the breeze.

When did I piss myself? he thought as he drove through the green lanes bathed in sunshine, until movement ahead caught his eye. He slowed instinctively, eyes narrowing as though that would help zoom his vision somehow, and he made out the shape of a person waving in a manner that screamed, 'not dead' at him. As he drew closer, the shape became a young woman, who stepped out into the road and continued to wave her arms frantically.

Nevin applied the brakes to come to a squeaking halt, looking down at a woman who was neither as young as he had first thought, nor as attractive as he had hoped. She was slightly thicker around the hips than he preferred, and her nose was too big for her face, but he reckoned that pickings would be slim nowadays.

And hell, who doesn't love a knight in shining armour? he told himself with a smirk he fought to keep hidden. Yanking on the handbrake, he climbed out and down to road level, leaving the submachine gun uselessly inside the Ferret.

"Oh, thank you," the woman gasped, "thank you for stopping, you've saved my life…" she bent over to rest her hands on her knees and catch her breath, "are there any more with you? Any more soldiers?" she asked as her nose wrinkled up at the smell of him, "There were a few of them chasing me," she said as she looked back over the hedge to the field on Nevin's left.

His gaze was drawn naturally to where the woman looked, and just as his head turned, a feeling of the empty air behind him suddenly filling spun him back around to find himself facing the black figure-eight of a shotgun muzzle.

"Hands up," growled a man with ragged facial hair, who held the gun pointed at him from a distance too close to be effective, yet close enough to be very intimidating. Nevin glanced back at the woman who was now smiling an evil sneer and holding a large hunting knife low in her right hand. Nevin smiled back at her, unsure why he felt so calm, given the situation, then back at the man pointing the shotgun at him.

And he chuckled again.

The chuckle got away from him, took on a life of its own and became a belly laugh that began to rumble and rise until he had totally lost it. Knife woman and shotgun man exchanged concerned looks and inched backwards involuntarily until they steeled themselves to challenge this laughing madman.

"Oi, dickhead," snarled shotgun man, "shut the fuck up before you attract attention to us all."

This only made Nevin laugh harder at the irony of the situation. Everything he had been through, everything he had survived and finally escaped, only to fall prey to pair of fucking amateurs at the classic 'damsel in distress' roadside blag. His laughter took on a tone describable only as *nasty,* and his eyes opened to check how far away both of them were from him. Something in his brain told him that the knife was far more dangerous to him than the shotgun was at the distances in play; that he only had to move a foot for the blast to miss him entirely but that the knife could find his soft belly in a heartbeat. All of the warrior potential inside him, everything that he could have been if only he had fitted in and applied himself, came boiling to the surface as he demonstrated the ability that others had seen hidden deep inside him.

Striking out like a snake he hit knife woman in the nose hard, snapping the punch back to make it a total shock instead of a knockout blow. As soon as he had lashed out, he stepped back, slapping his hand at the barrel of the shotgun to push it away from him just as the man pulled the trigger to blast a shot so close past knifewoman that she shrieked and threw herself down, where her legs seemed to furiously pedal an imaginary bicycle. Shotgun man's eyes went wide, and his mouth dropped open, thinking that he had killed her, though something in his expression made Nevin think it was fear of the consequences, as opposed to any genuine feeling of loss.

By the time he had regained his senses sufficiently to lift the barrel towards Nevin, he found himself staring into the much smaller but far steadier muzzle of a revolver aimed directly at his face. He froze, feeling the shotgun pulled from his grip as it dawned on him that he was beaten. The handgun disappeared from view as the wooden stock of his own gun arced upwards to hit him hard on the side of the head and spin him around to hit the ground, where he landed dizzy and disorientated but still conscious.

"You still alive?" Nevin asked the hissing, cursing woman who had stopped pedalling her legs and now sat up, rocking and holding her left flank where weak patches of blood showed through the material of her dirty T-shirt.

"You fucking *prick*," she snarled through gritted teeth as she fixed him with a look of utter loathing. Her breath came in gasps as though winded. "You... you *shot me!*"

"Technically," Nevin said conversationally, "*he's* the fucking prick who shot you. Now, I'll take all your supplies and the fuel from whatever vehicle you've got hidden around..."

His voice trailed away at a sound only half heard behind him. That sense made him freeze, tightening the grip on the revolver as his body tensed and he prepared to defend himself again. The tension locked him still as the sound solidified and grew into the unmistakable sound of a charging handle sliding back and forward to seat a bullet into a chamber. That sound made Nevin change his entire approach, switching from gloat-ingly dominant to obsequious and pathetic in an attempt to live through the situation.

"Okay, okay," he said, his hand releasing the grip on the weapon to let it dangle uselessly from his right index finger, "let's talk about this," he babbled, "to start with, they tried to ambush me, and secondly I didn't shoot her..."

"Shut your bloody mouth, Nevin," a gruff voice behind him said.

He shut his mouth, trying to place the voice and make sense of the turn of events.

"Sergeant... Sergeant Michaels?" he asked incredulously.

"Just Michaels will do," he said as he walked around him to stand over the bleeding woman and give her a blank look of disappointment, "I left that world," he said pointing a finger at Nevin's scout car, "behind me. I've got a different way now."

"So I see," Nevin said as he drew back up to his normal height and allowed the confidence back into his voice, "Do much ambushing of innocent people, do we?"

"Innocent?" Michaels asked, his eyes boring into Nevin like a shark's. "Nobody is *innocent* anymore; you're either alive or you're one of them."

He took a step closer to Nevin, putting his face uncomfortably close and not even recoiling when the smell hit him.

"Which one are you?" he asked, his gaze drilling into Nevin's eyes.

Nevin smiled again.

"I'm better at this shit than these two clowns are," he said evilly, gesturing at the two people still on the ground, "if you wanted someone better, that is…"

Michaels smiled at him as he stood back.

"Well then," he said, "welcome to my hilltop."

EPILOGUE

"Hello anybody," came the Liverpool accent over the radio, "this is the crew of the *Aunt Margaret* out of the Albert Docks. We have supplies and safety but are unable to put to sea because there are warships blockading the coast. If anyone can tell us where is safe to go, contact us on this frequency... Hello anybody, this is the crew of the *Aunt Margaret* out of the Albert Docks..."

"What do you think?" asked the man with his feet up on the wooden table over the sound of the wind howling outside. Despite the season being good, their location was prone to being battered by inclement weather at any time. When they did have fine sunshine and warm days, then the legions of tiny flies descended on them.

"I think we should tell them to sit tight for winter and then head up here. Tell them that the bastards won't survive the bad weather."

The man with his feet up said nothing, simply leaned forward with a groan and spun a dial to increase the microphone volume as he cleared his throat and put two fingers on the transmit button.

"Crew of the *Aunt Margaret*, come in," he said, waiting less than a heartbeat for an answer.

"We're here, hello? Who is this?"

"Crew of the *Aunt Margaret*," he said, ignoring the question, "listen carefully. The zombies will degrade over winter. Hold your ground if you can. Ration your supplies and just hold out until spring. I repeat, *hold your ground and ration supplies*. If you're still there in spring, we can talk. Out."

———

The two children walked through the familiar front door with obvious trepidation. Johnson went through first, his eyebrows raised and giving a soothing gesture with his right hand to Hampton. The eyebrows and the flat palm pressing downwards made the intention clear; *keep it calm.*

"Bill, Kimberley," he said in a voice they hadn't heard him use before as he glanced over at the injured woman, "this is Peter and Amber," he said as he stepped aside to reveal their two newest recruits, "and it looks like we might've moved into their house."

Hampton just beamed at them, completely unaware of how terrifying his gap-toothed grin appeared to them. Amber recoiled behind Peter slightly, glancing up the fair-skinned and blonde-haired Astrid with mixed admiration and trepidation.

"Kids," Johnson said as he bent down slightly in that condescending fashion that people adopt when they aren't used to children, "these are my friends, Bill," he pointed at the smiling marine sergeant with his swollen knee propped up on cushions, "and this is Kimberley."

From her position on the soft settee, her battered body bruised, and her leg bandaged, Kimberley brushed her hair over the scars on the left side of her face. She had given up on covering them in their company, knowing that what they had been through was far more important than her vanity, but it wasn't vanity that made her cover them now; children could be scared of her disfigurement and she wasn't of a mind to answer blunt questions.

Peter nodded at both of them, his face set in a grim approximation of seniority. He led Amber in by the hand, glancing back to see that the special forces sergeant had brought back the trolley of supplies, Bufford, responding to the look he received by dragging it through the door to prove that he hadn't failed at the task.

Enfield was still out there, bringing back the guns and supplies from the doorsteps of the houses they had already cleared. He came back, breaking the awkward silence by dropping the items inside and nodding to Bufford and Larsen, who both in turn looked back to Johnson.

"You're okay as a three?" Johnson asked, knowing that they were capable on their own and that he was likely their weakest link. Bufford said that they were, and led them out, to leave the atmosphere stilted and silent once more. Amber tugged at Peter's sleeve, leaning up to whisper in his ear. He pulled back, nodded at her, and slipped off his backpack to remove the shotgun, to watch as she reached into the bag and retrieved her ragged stuffed lamb. Peter held the gun with his fingertips, at no point wrapping his hand around the grip or going near the triggers, to show that he had no intention of using it.

When she had disappeared back upstairs, heading for the room they had occupied before and where she felt safe, Peter put the gun back in the bag, slipping off his shoes and shrugging out of his oversized jacket that he had thrown on inside out in his haste to flee the house. He walked straight into the kitchen, stopping to survey the empty cans and shoot a look at Johnson, before climbing up on the worktop and rising up on his knees to reach up and open the top window overlooking the secluded back garden. He disappeared into the utility area where the washing machine and dryer were, returning after a few seconds with a can of some non-descript fish and set it on the worktop, where he opened the second drawer down to pull out the can opener.

He punctured the thin metal, spinning the handle and squeezing out the oil into the drain in the sink before fetching a fork from the top drawer to scoop out the smelly contents into a shallow bowl.

Johnson jumped, his hand fluttering towards the weapon he had slung over his body, but then froze as the sound became a shape and that shape dropped onto the counter and let out a chippering meow of expectation. Peter slid the bowl towards the cat, who tucked in greedily and purred simultaneously.

"Was this your house, Peter?" Johnson asked, "I mean before."

"No," the boy replied simply.

Johnson paused, thinking how best to ask what he wanted to, in the end deciding to just ask it straight.

"What happened to you, kid?"

"How long have you got?" Peter asked, a small smile creeping across his face as he finally realised how much he had grown in such a short time.

———

The helicopter returned to the country house well before sunset, rushing their unconscious casualty inside past the two officers, who knew better than to shout for an explanation. The chief pilot, Barrett, nudged the arm of the SAS Major and both ducked into a ground floor study where the door was shut behind them.

Captain Palmer listened to the report in silence, his eyebrows only occasionally twitching before they were brought back under control, only speaking at the very end. He didn't insult their abilities to ask if they were sure about the island, or the downed aircraft, and especially not about the destruction witnessed at the base.

Trooper Povey will no doubt shed more unwelcome light on that matter, he told himself glumly, *assuming he recovers, that is.*

"Thank you, gentlemen," he said, walking to a dark wood bureau and pouring four measures of brandy into the bulbous, crystal glasses. He used the pause to think, to frame the words he needed to say in such a way that the others understood what he meant to achieve. He handed out the glasses to each man in turn and resumed his original place, before looking them all in the eye and swirling the glass in his hand before raising it.

"To our fallen," he said solemnly.

"*To our fallen,*" the others echoed quietly before they all took a long pull of their drinks. From any other man, such a formal display would have run the risk of appearing forced, unnatural or even laughable. From Julian Palmer it just seemed right somehow.

"Gentlemen," he said again in a more resolved tone, "we have an uncertain time ahead of us, to put matters mildly. We have lost more than half of our original fighting strength. We have almost one hundred civilians who are in need of organising and protecting, not to mention feeding. We have a matter of weeks before we are into autumn and that ticking clock runs straight into winter. We have power, but we need to consider food and fuel in addition to defences," he paused to sip his brandy once more, "In short, chaps," he said with a hint of a smile, "we've got a lot to do in a short space of time if we have any hope of surviving this."

The other eyes in the room met his, none of them missing the severity of his point.

"As far as I see," Palmer finished, "we can expect nothing in the way of assistance or outside help. Make no mistake, gentlemen: we have been abandoned."

ALSO IN THE SERIES

Toy Soldiers:

Apocalypse

Aftermath

You just read: Abandoned

Up next: Adversity

Books five and six yet to be named (coming 2019)

SPECIAL THANKS TO:

ADAWIA E. ASAD
JENNY AVERY
BARDE PRESS
CALUM BEAULIEU
BEN
BECKY BEWERSDORF
BHAM
TANNER BLOTTER
ALFRED JOSEPH BOHNE IV
CHAD BOWDEN
ERREL BRAUDE
DAMIEN BROUSSARD
CATHERINE BULLINER
JUSTIN BURGESS
MATT BURNS
BERNIE CINKOSKE
MARTIN COOK
ALISTAIR DILWORTH
JAN DRAKE
BRET DULEY
RAY DUNN
ROB EDWARDS
RICHARD EYRES
MARK FERNANDEZ
CHARLES T FINCHER
SYLVIA FOIL
GAZELLE OF CAERBANNOG
DAVID GEARY
MICHEAL GREEN
BRIAN GRIFFIN

EDDIE HALLAHAN
JOSH HAYES
PAT HAYES
BILL HENDERSON
JEFF HOFFMAN
GODFREY HUEN
JOAN QUERALTÓ IBÁÑEZ
JONATHAN JOHNSON
MARCEL DE JONG
KABRINA
PETRI KANERVA
ROBERT KARALASH
VIKTOR KASPERSSON
TESLAN KIERINHAWK
ALEXANDER KIMBALL
JIM KOSMICKI
FRANKLIN KUZENSKI
MEENAZ LODHI
DAVID MACFARLANE
JAMIE MCFARLANE
HENRY MARIN
CRAIG MARTELLE
THOMAS MARTIN
ALAN D. MCDONALD
JAMES MCGLINCHEY
MICHAEL MCMURRAY
CHRISTIAN MEYER
SEBASTIAN MÜLLER
MARK NEWMAN
JULIAN NORTH

KYLE OATHOUT
LILY OMIDI
TROY OSGOOD
GEOFF PARKER
NICHOLAS (BUZ) PENNEY
JASON PENNOCK
THOMAS PETSCHAUER
JENNIFER PRIESTER
RHEL
JODY ROBERTS
JOHN BEAR ROSS
DONNA SANDERS
FABIAN SARAVIA
TERRY SCHOTT
SCOTT
ALLEN SIMMONS
KEVIN MICHAEL STEPHENS
MICHAEL J. SULLIVAN
PAUL SUMMERHAYES
JOHN TREADWELL
CHRISTOPHER J. VALIN
PHILIP VAN ITALLIE
JAAP VAN POELGEEST
FRANCK VAQUIER
VORTEX
DAVID WALTERS JR
MIKE A. WEBER
PAMELA WICKERT
JON WOODALL
BRUCE YOUNG

CPSIA information can be obtained
at www.ICGtesting.com
Printed in the USA
BVHW031531070521
606757BV00003B/353

9 781949 890396